THE CARES OF THE DAY

THE CARES OF THE DAY

IVAN WEBSTER

FICTION
COLLECTIVE
T W O

BOULDER · NORMAL

This book is the winner of the 1994 Charles H. and
N. Mildred Nilon Excellence in Minority Fiction Award,
sponsored by the University of Colorado and
Fiction Collective Two

Published jointly by the University of Colorado and Fiction
Collective Two with assistance from
                the Illinois Arts Council and the support of
the Publications Center of the University of Colorado at
Boulder and the Unit for Contemporary Literature at Illinois
State University

Address all inquiries to: Fiction Collective Two, Publications
Center, Campus Box 494, University of Colorado, Boulder,
CO 80309-0494

The Cares of the Day
Ivan Webster

ISBN, Cloth: 0-932511-89-9, $21.95
ISBN, Paper: 0-932511-90-2, $10.95

Manufactured in the United States of America
Distributed by the Talman Company

To ANITA ADDISON, BEVERLEE BRUCE *and* CHARLOTTE CARTER

—black women extraordinaire

Why should it be my loneliness,
Why should it be my song,
Why should it by my dream
      deferred
        overlong?

—Langston Hughes
"Tell Me"

THE CARES OF THE DAY
FAMILY TREE

(with the ages of the characters when the book opens in 1957)

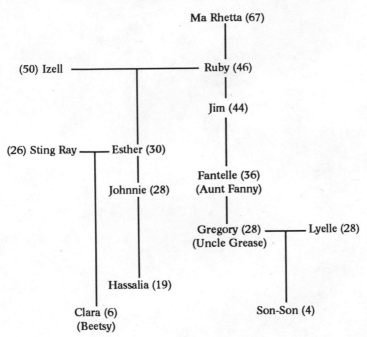

Ma Rhetta (67)

(50) Izell —————————— Ruby (46)

Jim (44)

(26) Sting Ray —┬— Esther (30)

Johnnie (28)

Fantelle (36)
(Aunt Fanny)

Gregory (28) ————— Lyelle (28)
(Uncle Grease)

Hassalia (19)

Clara (6)
(Beetsy)

Son-Son (4)

PART ONE

HASSALIA, 1957

Sit where the light corrupts your face.

—Gwendolyn Brooks
"In the Mecca"

WE JUST CAME ON IN THE HOUSE when we got back from laying Ma Rhetta away. Walking up to the house Esther swung her hips like she'd been wanting to all day. She got out of the car first. It was one of Jim's old beat-up Buicks. He had different cars all the time. If Ma Rhetta woulda died two weeks sooner we'da gone to her burying in a beat-up green Cadillac. Before that it woulda been a blue DeSoto. Jim didn't care what he was riding in as long as he wasn't walking. And he didn't care what the inside of the car smelled like—wet, nasty rugs, wine, some of no telling whose funk—as long as it was moving.

Unless it was in the wintertime, Jim always rode with the windows open. After he turned on the keys, first thing he did was put on the radio, even before he started the motor. And the last thing he did when he got out was turn the radio off. When you rode with Jim, you were always talking over noise: jump music, or Ernie Banks hitting a home run or the Chicago Bears running up and down. You had to talk loud even when you didn't feel loud.

It was wet and cold that October Friday. Jim drove careful 'cause the leaves falling made the road slick. Ma Rhetta passed that Tuesday before. She was bad sick, and the doctor came three times that day. Old Dr. Clay. White man. White hair. Always a blue suit, black bag, brown hat he took off the minute he hit the door. He told Mama there wasn't any reason to move Ma Rhetta to the hospital. Said there wasn't much to do. Move her, we might lose her. She failed, he said. That's how doctors, even white doctors, would say it. "Ruby"—Mama used to do housework for him and Mrs. Clay—"your mother is failing." Back in August, that was the first thing out of his mouth after he looked up under Ma Rhetta's eyelids and listened at her breasts and held her wrists. When he touched one of us when we were sick we would always talk after he left how gentle his hands were. We didn't expect it from a white man. He held Ma Rhetta's hand like it was a baby's, and when he finished he closed her fingers back into a little ball.

He told Mama to keep her warm, get her to eat what we could and don't let her out of bed (said he was going to send his nurse by later with a bedpan for us to borrow). Ma Rhetta was down real sick for a couple of months before she died.

After the first week she couldn't talk.

"Stroke, Doctor?" Mama said.

"Sort of like, Ruby. What has happened is, your mother's brain won't tell her arms and legs what to do. We could move her to a hospital and feed her through a tube and have nurses watching her all the time, and bathing her, but her brain still wouldn't talk to her arms and her legs. She's comfortable here, as long as all of you can watch her and talk to her and turn her in the bed every once in a while, and give her a good bath morning and evening. I'll look in."

So, that's what Mama and me did. With help, kind of, from Esther. Mama and me had sense enough not to ask Esther to help too much. Esther could watch the water heat and tell us when it was ready. But it would be all over the linoleum in the kitchen if we asked her to put it on to heat. Or spilled all the way up the stairs if she brought it to Ma Rhetta's room. Pouring boiling hot water from a bucket into a pan, cooling it off with some cold, and then carrying it up

14

the stairs with a wash rag and soap, without burning herself or Beetsy or Ma Rhetta—who, 'cause of the stroke, couldna even told Esther, "Girl, you're burning me," but woulda had to scream before Esther would understand that water next to a 67-year-old woman who's bad sick has to be warm to do her any good, but not scalding hot—all of that was too complicated for Esther, even if the woman she was tending was her grandmother.

Aunt Lyelle came over every few days. But we were lucky to get five words or fifteen minutes out of her before she said she had to get back to Son-Son, her and Uncle Grease's big little boy. He wasn't in kindergarten yet, big as he was, 'cause he was still only four. Lyelle would slide in the door, skinny as one of her Camel cigarettes, come upstairs and stand there staring at Ma Rhetta while Mama or me would go out in the back yard and knock some green apples out of the tree to fry for Ma Rhetta's breakfast, or run down to Talbot's for a loaf of bread or a half a gallon of milk. Before we'd get back good from whatever we had to do, Lyelle woulda slid down the steps and out the front door. Blue Camel smoke on the stairs was the only way you knew she was ever there.

Mama said she didn't want Ma Rhetta left alone, not in the daytime. So it was me or her. Summertime, and I already graduated from high school. Sometimes we'd wheel in M'Lady. She could walk but mostly sat in a wheelchair and wasn't right in her mind, and she didn't say anything any way. Never did. We'd turn her toward Ma Rhetta. Ma Rhetta could see M'Lady because I could see Ma Rhetta squinch her eyes and blink when I rolled M'Lady's wheelchair up next to the bed. But M'Lady just sighed and looked out the window or stared at the pitcher of water next to Ma Rhetta's bed. Or just looked off into space.

She was past 80 when Ma Rhetta told Mama to take her in six months before. We never knew why. And Mama wouldn't argue with Ma Rhetta about it. She just did it.

So M'Lady wasn't really help. She was just comp'ny watching Ma Rhetta dying.

I didn't think that was what Ma Rhetta was doing. I knew she was awful bad sick, but I believed she would get back up out of that bed and come down those steps and say to me, "Hassalia, why a girl like you won't put on a skirt and blouse and stop wearin' those overhalls is more foolishness than I can see. We called you Little Man since you wasn't much bigger than Beetsy, the time you put on Izell's hat and strutted around here like you had somewhere to go. All of five or six years old you was, near as I can remember. And all mouth. But, Little Man, you can come out those pants now and act like some kind of little ol' girl around here any time you ready."

She would stop and look at me and let me think about what she said. They all told me every day to stop wearing overhalls and put on a skirt. So I stood there and looked like I wasn't thinking about it—but like I was thinking about it, too. I had to get a little of that in there or Ma Rhetta would call me out to Mama, say I was completely disrespectful, and the next minute Mama would be on me, too. So I stood there like I was thinking about wearing a skirt and like I wasn't. And finally Ma Rhetta would say, "Any time you ready" over again, real polite. Like she would wait 'til I was 107 if that was how long it was gonna take. The skirt was her business, she was telling me, the foolishness was mine. "Any time you ready," she would say one more time, and go on in the kitchen and help Mama peel potatoes for supper, leaving me standing there with nothing to say, since I wasn't ready and didn't know when I was gonna be ready. And I knew I was a girl anyway.

I still wasn't ready to put on a skirt in the fall of 1957. But you couldna told me Ma Rhetta would die before I would be.

Ma Rhetta was somebody to me before I knew what somebody meant. It was hard when she was just gone like that. Seemed like she went into the air. I couldn't look anywhere in the house that October without thinking I'd see her shuffling around in her slippers, wearing an old housecoat or an apron, or both of 'em at the same time—helping out or waiting for a chance to go back to bed. Ma Rhetta had her good days and her bad days long before she got bad sick.

She was the one named me Little Man. My name is Hassalia. Ever since I don't know when people been calling me Has. Not has, like you got something. It's Has, with a hiss on the end of it, like a snake. I been skinny since I was little, and Mama found some money to buy me glasses from when I wasn't but five or six. I didn't want to keep 'em on, but Mama made me. Said she paid for 'em.

Those glasses were why Ma Rhetta called me Little Man that time I put on my Daddy's hat and started walking around the house. I looked like a little man, Ma Rhetta said. And everybody started calling me Little Man, teasing me.

After a while I knew they weren't always teasing me. That was what they called me when they wanted to jump on my nerves.

*

Esther. "Little Man, why don't you come out of those overhalls and act like some kind of woman? With your bulldagger-looking self, I don't know what folks are s'posed to think. You trying to scare somebody, Has, with your skinny, mannish self? Running around here in some ol' piece of leather you call a aviator jacket. It's something Jim gave you from outta all of his junk. Nobody in this world knows where he gets all of that junk. And you don't think nothing of putting it on and wearing it 'cause it makes you

17

look like some shif'less bum off the street. Come from nowhere and nobody knows where you going. You're trying to be like that piece of man jumped off the train last week Mama fed out on the back porch. Beetsy wasn't scared, but I've got a baby girl ain't scared of nothing. I was scared, but Mama's baby wasn't, were you, Beetsy, sugar? See, Has, now this little chile of mine got her some nerve, you understand what I'm saying? She just went right out on the porch and stood there and watched that man eat that plate full of grits and gravy Mama gave him. Ate like he didn't eat nothing for days. Jumping on and off trains! Mama's little Sugar Beet went right up to him and asked him where he was from and where he was going. Said he was from 'Way yonder' and going 'Down the line'. Down the line! Railroad nigger going down that ol' railroad line to Chicago, where he was gon' beg on the streets. And you, Has, around here looking like something the train left, in overhalls, beat up tennis shoes and a leather jacket. I don't know what you think you look like, Hassalia, but, girl, I wish you could see yourself. Ain't no man gon' be following behind no woman dresses like him and talks like him, all low down in your throat, like you might go up 'side his head if he jumps wrong. You're just acting out, Little Man, that's all you're doing."

✳

Jim. "Had me a dream last night. Sit down, Little Man. I ain't s'posed to be having no dreams. I don't have 'em. But I did last night. Sit down, Hassalia. Mama up there dying and I'm in my room down the hall, dreaming.

"I was under water. In a house. Me and Mama. House full of water. And me and Mama could talk. She was laid up in bed, like she is now. But she had more life in her. I was standing by the door, standing guard against some sharks I thought was coming in there after us. These sharks was swimming by the window, but they couldn't get in. They was too big. They showed their teeth and rolled their eyes right outside the windows. Mama told me not to be scared. She said, 'Son, those sharks don't fancy you. Stop your foolishness, boy.' Then Mama let go of all her water. Right there in the bed. There wasn't no smell or nothing. She smiled and looked at me and said, 'Boy, go on and open that door. Your Daddy coming back and you not gon' open the door and let him in?' She laughed, and closed back up her legs and threw the blanket on herself. There were fishes and things swimming by, but we could breathe all right.

"The water was green but it wasn't cold. And didn't no bubbles come out our mouths. Somebody knocked on the door, and Mama said, 'Boy, go on and let your Daddy in.' I went to the door and opened it and it was a shark out there. I said, 'Mama, I don't want this shark to come in.' Shark showing his teeth and cutting his eyes at me. He waiting at the door for me to let him in. Mama say, 'Boy, that fish is just trying to be your friend. What's wrong with you?'

"Right then, while that shark was banging up against the house, Mama got a pain in her belly and start to crying. I said 'Mama, don't cry. I'll take care of you. I'll get the doctor.' She say, 'Boy, it's too late for that. The doctor ain't gon' get by that shark. It's too late, boy. It's too late.'

"Then right there on the bed, Mama turned into a big blue fish with a long tail and a mouth full of big teeth. She started to cry again. She said, 'Boy, I'm sorry. It hurts me to do it, but I got to.' She swam off the bed and over to me and wrapped that tail around me and pinned me down and bit her teeth into my side. Lawd, it hurt.

"I could see in her eyes she was sorry and didn't want to hurt me. As soon as her teeth sunk into my side real good— it hurt bad right that minute, but I knew I'd be all right. I knew she *wasn't* all right. Wasn't gon' *be* all right.

"She picked me up and put me on the bed with that tail of hers, and pulled a big chunk of my side out of me, just ripped me wide open and saw me bleed. She had part of me in her mouth. Then she let go of me. The bottom of the house fell off, and there wasn't nothing down there but deep, dark ocean. Mama sank, real slow, down into the ocean, with that piece of me, bleeding, in her mouth. She was crying. Her eyes stared back up at me. All the way down. 'Til I couldn't see her no more. I had a big hole in me. But I knew I would be all right. All the way down I kept seeing her eyes, crying, and that piece of me in her mouth, bleeding. My side hurt bad. Then I woke up."

✴

I'm gonna be a wheel some day
I'm gonna be somebody
I'm gonna be a real gone cat
And then I won't want you

Fats Domino was singing on the radio when we were coming back to the house. I felt bad. Jim kept it on. I couldn't stop thinking about Ma Rhetta down there in the ground where we left her.

Sting Ray came back not too long after Ma Rhetta died. Turned out to be the next to last time. At first when we put Ma Rhetta away, everything got quiet. But by the time Sting Ray showed up something was happening. Ma Rhetta was gone and him and everybody else started acting completely crazy. The whole house came apart that fall. When I look back now, it's hard for me to believe the whole thing only took that summer and fall. It was October when Ma Rhetta died. By November Sting Ray was back and driving all of us nearly as crazy as he was.

But maybe we were already going crazy and didn't know

it. It was strange what Ma Rhetta's passing did. Jim with his nightmares was only the beginning. Jim kind of took over. Ma Rhetta musta left this space in the house, inside Jim, that he didn't know was there until she was gone. Didn't any of us know what was there. We all did the craziest things, trying to fill up that space. Maybe Sting Ray was just the craziest one of us. But I swear that damn nigger had a head start, I'm not lying to you.

We lived on a corner where three streets came together. One street was in front of our house and the other one was in back. The third one was on the side. So our yard was the whole block. It was a short block, but still pretty big, and our yard, especially in the back, was bigger than most people's. But you ask anybody in Crawley, white or black, and they'd tell you we had the littlest yard. It seemed like that to folks 'cause they didn't come in it. And they didn't come in it 'cause it was full of junk. We had the junkiest yard in Crawley. I knew that. Told myself I didn't care what people said. Jim bought and sold all kinds of stuff, and he had to keep it out in the yard. Didn't have any place else to keep it. Washing machines, refrigerators, sinks, tubs, typewriters, books, baskets, steel drums, tires, lawn mowers, hoses, pots and pans, dishes, living room and bedroom furniture, rugs rolled up or hung on clotheslines to be beat, chifforobes (some of 'em full of old clothes—good clothes), barrels full of nails, old cars, pieces of old cars, all kinda tools for working on cars, all kinda pipes to do plumbing, fishing poles, handmade combs from over in Europe and Africa, all kinda flower pots and birdbaths and pink flamingoes and statues of colored jockeys from out of folks' yards, screwdrivers, cans of paint, Mason jars of vegetables and jelly that somebody gave to Jim for something else, parts of tractors, a chicken coop full of chickens Jim was moving for somebody so they would do him a favor, barbecues, televisions, big black skillets, wash tubs, ice buckets, pieces of fresh cut

21

lumber, rakes, hoes, television antennas, curtain rods, hot combs, red coffee grinding machines from the A&P, sets of wrenches, vises, trellises for people's flowers to climb on, pie plates, hat racks, hunting knives, storm windows, paint brushes, hammers, bags full of marbles, toilet bowls, toasters, sets of hairbrushes, big radios and little radios, flashlights, iron porch railings, pliers, model trains, propellers from offa boats, pruning shears, wire cutters, lawn trimmers, stacks of records, handsaws and chain saws, lathes, furnaces (whole, round furnaces, with all the pipes and flues to go with 'em), all kinda scissors, ice picks, fence-pole diggers, bags of clothespins, trowels, bath mats, rolls of linoleum, watering cans, scrub brushes, fish tanks, all kinda salt and pepper shakers, canister sets, thermometers, mirrors, heavy iron lawn furniture, wood and aluminum step ladders, pianos, horseshoes and all like that.

He kept some of this stuff under tar paper sheds along the edge of the back yard by the fence. He had old army tents that he could lay 'cross the front of the sheds for when it rained, and corrugated roofing on the floor so the water that did get in would run off. He had good pianos and trunks full of fine clothes and all kinda crystal and china down in the basement, and expensive rugs and drapes and things he wouldn't tell us about. Jim was a junk man. And he was my uncle. And I didn't let anybody mess with me about it.

Ma Rhetta never had a husband. She had four children, all with different daddies: Mama, Jim, Aunt Fanny and Uncle Grease. Uncle Grease's right name was Gregory, but they started calling him Grease from when he was little because he was always so slow. Him and Aunt Lyelle still took all day to do anything. Nobody believed they would have a baby, both of 'em so tall and skinny and slow-talking you wouldna thought they could make up their minds to it. But somehow they had Son-Son, and he turned out to be a giant. Gregory and Aunt Lyelle didn't live too far from us. But when we'd call them it would always take them the longest time to get to our house. Uncle Grease worked nights over at the electrical plant, assembling parts with a soldering iron. He was home all day. Seemed like he never did sleep. I used to think maybe that was why he was so slow. But he was slow from a boy, Mama told me.

Things happened funny, and that was hard on Gregory. Mama was 16 when she and my Daddy, Izell, had Esther. Two years after that they had my brother Johnnie. But Ma Rhetta wasn't through, either. Same time Mama was carrying Johnnie, Ma Rhetta was carrying Gregory. Johnnie was born a week before Uncle Grease. So Uncle Grease was Johnnie's uncle, but Johnnie was older than him. Esther was, too, but she was a girl. What was hard on Gregory was, him and Johnnie grew up together and Johnnie was first in everything.

All you'd have to do was look at a picture of Johnnie and you'd see why. Let me tell you, my brother Johnnie was one handsome man. I mean, you talk about fine, you're talking about Johnnie. Full, curly head of black hair, prettiest brown skin you'd ever wanna see, sweet eyes, shiny teeth and a way of walking and talking that was so smooth you just got on outta his way.

Johnnie never did pay attention to any school teacher or anybody like that. Said he wasn't gonna 'cause he knew he was gonna be somebody from jump. He could play him some basket*ball*, ooo wee! The white girls over at the high school were crazy about him. But Johnnie wasn't fool enough to be crazy back.

See, Johnnie loved music. He just knew he was gonna be a singer like Nat King Cole or Sam Cooke or Jackie Wilson. Johnnie was the biggest fool about Nat. Would sit upstairs and listen to Nat's records for hours. Said his voice was higher than Nat's, maybe even prettier, but Johnnie knew there was nobody mellower or smoother than Nat King

Cole. And Nat could play him some piano. Johnnie loved that even more than the way he sang—the way Nat could play a piano. Johnnie started singing at church, and the choir leader told him she thought he could sing real well. He left church and started listening to Nat, and before too long that was that. He knew what he was gonna do. He was going to Chicago and sing. And going on from there to New York, and all over the world. Just like Nat.

Uncle Grease was nothing like Nat King Cole. Uncle Grease was nothing like Johnnie. There the two of 'em were, Mama told me, and it seemed like Johnnie was always out in front. Johnnie was riding a bicycle when Gregory couldn't stay up on one. Johnnie played baseball hard and fast and Gregory could never swing the bat right. Johnnie got picked for all the teams at school and nobody wanted Gregory. Johnnie was the one all the girls wanted to dance with at parties. Gregory stood against the wall, and then stopped going. Gregory was clumsy and tripped all over his feet. One afternoon on a bet Johnnie beat the whole track team in a 50-yard dash without even warming up.

All this was hard on Gregory. Too hard, Mama said. Ma Rhetta knew what Gregory was going through, too, but she loved to see Johnnie run and clown and dance, just like the rest of us did. Johnnie was Gregory's nephew, but Gregory didn't feel like he was ahead of him in anything.

So Gregory got old. By the time he was 17, Gregory was acting like everything was all over and settled. The way he came up on Lyelle (her people moved to Crawley from Louisiana) and married her was the way the two of them would always be together, peculiar. When they met, Lyelle wasn't but 17 herself. According to Mama, neither one of 'em knew what to do with themselves after school, with anybody, black or white. They just kinda fell into walking home together, but nobody thought anything about it they both seemed so pitiful.

Lyelle was tall and skinny, and had creamy brown skin, same color as Gregory's. But she didn't know how to dress a little bit, Mama said, never did. Her daddy was a jackleg preacher who didn't put up with a whole lot of dressing up and lipstick and all of that. He delivered coal in the wintertime and plowed fields with a tractor in the spring and mowed lawns and cut weeds in the summer. He was a backbreaker, the way Mama used to say, give him that. He would help out at the church and time by time they would let him preach.

Lyelle and her mother would come to church and sit there, both of 'em dressed in white, and afterwards they'd gather up Lyelle's daddy, and the three of 'em would just go on home. They looked holy, but they didn't stand around so nobody knew if they really were or not.

After she got outta school Lyelle got a job in the ten cent store, one of the first colored, and she kept it for quite a while because the man said he hardly knew she was there. She was a stockgirl in the back. She kept track of ribbons and buttons and needles and thread and yarn and all that kinda stuff. She could sew from early on, and she could always make extra money that way. So Gregory, getting older by the minute the way he thought, saw him some Lyelle and decided—decided we don't know what, Mama would say, laughing. Ma Rhetta would be listening and she'd always laugh at this part, too.

Lyelle talked proper and would say things like, "Yes, Ma'm" and "Thank you, Ma'm, I certainly will tell Mama and Daddy you asked after 'em" and "No, Ma'm, I wasn't planning on going back to school, thank you for asking. What I'm trying to learn is how to get by after Mama and Daddy pass on, being alone in this world like I will be, and the white folks' school doesn't have classes in that. I don't know what I will do with what they are telling me. Where am I going to *be* a secretary—even after I get some more schooling—in Crawley or anyplace else?" She made good sense, sorta.

But nobody could figure out how her and Gregory got the idea they would get married. What did they think was coming together?

One thing folks knew: Lyelle wasn't pregnant. Nobody was sure she and Gregory even knew how all o' that went. You could barely get the two of 'em to go to the Sunday school picnic together. They would sit around together, by themselves, and hardly even talk. What did they know about getting married or having babies? Well, it took 'em six years to have Son-Son. And when he finally came, all 12 pounds of him, the two of 'em took so long to name him that 'til he was full grown hardly anybody ever used his real name, which is Luther. But Son-Son had to find a way to live with a lot more than just his name after that fall.

It was after Ma Rhetta passed that we had to figure out what to do to see after Aunt Fanny, too. Course we never knew exactly what to do for her, not since she was 20-something and sorta lost her mind. Poor Aunt Fanny. I would go by Gregory's and see her a lot. That's where she stayed after she left our house and wouldn't come back. Ma Rhetta tried to make her come back, but it wasn't any use. Finally everybody gave up and let her stay at Uncle Grease's. Sometimes I would take something Mama baked or brought home from her white folks'. Other times it was a dress, or something nice Jim had on the truck I asked him for for Aunt Fanny.

Ma Rhetta and Mama and Jim and even Daddy acted like they were kinda ashamed of Aunt Fanny, and I didn't think it was right. Aunt Fanny didn't ever hurt anybody and wasn't intending to hurt anybody. It wasn't her fault if that soldier didn't want to marry her and was never even thinking of marrying her. I used to make Mama tell me about it. Aunt Fanny was her sister, after all. And I wanted to know. But Mama didn't like to talk about it. She said Fanny acted a fool over a man who couldna meant her no good at all. And didn't have anything to be a fool over but the uniform on his back.

A soldier. That's what Fanny fell for. A *white* soldier. What kind of fool did Fanny think the man was? *She* was the fool. And, Mama said, it ran her out of her mind.

Aunt Fanny was a sorta paid volunteer during World War II down at the courthouse. USO folks were there shipping things overseas to the soldiers and writing letters to 'em. They were glad enough to have colored help 'em out, especially since there weren't all that many colored troops from Crawley then. And when the colored came home on furlough, they didn't go to white USO parties anyway. They just came home and stayed with their people, like they knew the Crawley white folks wanted 'em to. The Army was segregated, so relaxing time when the soldiers got home was the same way. That was fine.

Aunt Fanny wasn't down there helping the folks pack boxes of cookies. They didn't want colored help with *that*. She only went down to USO parties to serve and help clean up. She wasn't a hostess for the white troops, and she knew it. She sure wasn't that big a fool. She worked in the kitchen. Because she could use the money.

Aunt Fanny didn't have a husband. She was still young and she maybe coulda got one, but nobody really thought she would. Aunt Fanny was too nervous was all anybody could say. She was. She wasn't pretty, either. Aunt Fanny had buck teeth and big eyes and was all arms and legs. She was tall, kinda like me. Mama said she shoulda known not to be such a fool.

She was working back in the kitchen in the courthouse basement when this white soldier comes in. And he stops and stands there sipping on his punch, and talks to her right there in the kitchen. The white USO ladies come out and start to see what's going on and they tell this soldier boy maybe he should come back into the main hall and drink his punch out there. And he politely tells 'em he's fine where he is and they can just go back out in the hall.

Aunt Fanny sees what's going on—or, Mama used to wonder, did she?—and she doesn't tell the white soldier boy he'd better go back in with his own and she'd stay out in the kitchen with the dishes. Turns out this soldier boy was from somewhere in Texas and was on his way back there when he stopped off in Crawley with some soldier friend of his.

Some kinda way, he talked Aunt Fanny into running off with him that night. When they got as far as Kansas City, he was through with her. They stayed in some lowdown kinda hotel in the colored section there, and after that they were headed God knew where. Whatever he was telling Fanny. But it was right there in Kansas City he just left her on a bench in the train station. Picked up his duffel back and said he was going to the men's and wash up and would be right back and didn't come back. That's what we found out later. It took the police there three days—after they picked her up, screaming all over the station—before they got her right name out of her, she was so ashamed and scared. The police said at first she got away from 'em and ran outta the train station looking all up and down for the soldier before they got hold of her and took her to the police station. Where her and him stayed and what they did for ten days running before he left her Mama and Ma Rhetta only found out a little bit at a time, much later, long after Aunt Fanny got back. In all o' that Kansas City craziness, the police finally got a message to Ma Rhetta, and her and Mama got word to Daddy. He had friends on the railroad who were running through Kansas City right then, and they helped him pick up Aunt Fanny and bring her home.

She didn't say anything for weeks after she got back. Not a word. Ma Rhetta called her every kinda fool, but Mama said Aunt Fanny didn't really hear her. She just sat in the house in a living-room chair and didn't say anything to anybody.

Real slow, she got herself back to living among folks and seeing people and going to church and all. But she was never completely all right in her head. And she wouldn't talk about what happened to her except in a way you had to figure out what she meant. You could if you knew. She would talk about trains, and if you knew you knew, she was thinking about that soldier. And you would think maybe she was thinking about a trip she took somewhere nice, but if you knew, you knew she was thinking about what that soldier did with her before he decided he had enough and just left her, a tall, small-town colored woman from Illinois, in Kansas, not knowing how she got there or how she was gonna get back home. And I would start to hate that soldier.

But then I would remember that Aunt Fanny was always kind of nervous. I was little when this happened and I didn't understand about it then, but I can remember her being nervous. And I remember her walking around the house when she got back and not being able to talk to anybody. I thought she was sick. But she never really changed. She was nervous all the time. She just got *more* nervous after that soldier. She couldn't go anywhere for long by herself. Folks colored and white in Crawley started to know she wasn't s'posed to be out too long by herself, so they'd look at her funny when she walked in a store and they'd start to wonder whether she was staying out longer than she was s'posed to and should they be trying to find Jim and tell him to come and get her. She didn't really walk far, ever. But nobody knew what she was s'posed to do, and she didn't look like what she was telling you was the truth anyway. So nobody said anything to her except, "How are you today, Fanny?" and "That sure is a handsome hat, Fanny." And the truth was, after that soldier Aunt Fanny lost her mind.

We didn't say it just like that for years, until one night she stayed out 'til all hours, and somebody found her way out by the lake walking around in her nightgown with no shoes. Mama said nobody even knew she was out of the house. When the police brought her home that time Ma Rhetta said she wasn't gonna have it. Blessed her out but good. Aunt Fanny burst into tears and ran out the door and up the street—with everybody watching 'cause it was the middle of the day by then—to Uncle Grease's house.

Him and Lyelle took her in. She said she wanted to stay with them, that Ma Rhetta hated her and that Mama wouldn't help her. Gregory and Lyelle weren't sure what to do. They let her stay 'cause they didn't want her to go back down the street again in front of all the neighbors, even if somebody was walking with her this time. She upset the whole neighborhood.

Ma Rhetta told me to take some clothes down there to her. I was 13 by then, and I carried them down there in four or five trips, by myself. Ma Rhetta didn't want anybody else doing anything. Uncle Grease and Aunt Lyelle didn't have that big a place, but it was big enough, so Aunt Fanny stayed there. And after a while Ma Rhetta would go down there and see her, and Mama and me got so we would go all the time.

After that, Aunt Fanny calmed down for a little while. She turned out to be a big help after Son-Son was born and kept growing like he did. The way it turned out, sometimes Aunt Fanny would kinda play in her mind Son-Son was the little boy she and that soldier had. Gregory and Lyelle didn't care. Son-Son was like three or four children. It didn't bother them what Aunt Fanny called him while she made bread pudding for him.

Mama was the first one showed me how, if you listened to Aunt Fanny real close while she was talking to Son-Son—who was big, but, still, just a chile—you could tell she was playing like Son-Son was the soldier, then like he was the baby the two of 'em mighta had, and then she'd turn him into the soldier again. You'd go over there and Gregory and Lyelle would be at different ends of the house not saying anything, and in the middle of the living room floor Aunt Fanny and Son-Son would be playing soldier or playing with toy trains and making up stories together and unless you knew, most of it didn't make much sense.

*

Daddy's name was Izell. Mama kept a picture of him on her dresser in her bedroom. Daddy stayed gone. Left out when I was little. He wrote now and again, and sometimes he even called up on the telephone. I talked to him. But after I got up past seven, we never saw him anymore. He used to write and tell me he wanted to see me. But he never got through Crawley, he said, and I believed him. He worked on the railroad and went all around the country. Him and Mama had Esther and then Johnnie and then, after a while, me. After me, he left.

A hundred times I asked Mama why, and she always told me Daddy couldn't stay put. Was a traveling man when she met him. Started on the railroad when he was a boy and never in his heart left it. He would stop once in a while to do some common work—digging trenches for the city sewage lines, hauling trash, mixing concrete. But he'd get tired of the heat and the dirt and head back for the road, where, even if the work wasn't always cleaner, the money might be better and the times were bound to be. Mama said once he got to be a Pullman porter he started bringing his railroad friends by the house and they would talk about St. Louis and Memphis and New York and Kansas City and all the fine clothes and people and good times, and Mama just sat there listening to 'em all. Daddy never talked about taking Mama with him, at least not very far. Time by time, she told me, they'd go into Chicago and dance a little or see a show, but he was just showing her a taste of it all, he used to say. The road was where it all was. She figured out quick enough "the road" meant women, too.

And for a lot of years when she would tell people Daddy was on the road they looked at her funny, like what kinda fool could she be. Then, she said, they stopped looking at her funny, 'cause she stopped talking like she ever expected Daddy to come back. When he did, she got to the point where she damn sure didn't expect him to stay. He sent her some money once in a while, and there were a whole lot of colored men in Crawley who weren't doing one bit better than he was, and their women got respected at the church just'cause the men were around. Mama said it wasn't right. Leastwise, that's how she explained it to me when I got up to enough size to beg to know where my daddy was and why.

But when I was little, I used to just miss him. I used to say, "When my daddy comes, he'll sock you in the nose," or, "My daddy's gon' buy me that jackknife, you wait and see," or "My daddy gon' take me to the carnival next time he's here." That's the kinda stuff I said to other people sometimes when they got on my nerves.

When I was by myself I used to think about my daddy a lot. He used to come and take me away on horses, and we'd fly together and dance together and laugh so hard we'd fall on the floor. And I talked to him, too. I didn't tell anybody. But I used to go out in the woods and find places just to talk to him when there was something I had to tell him. Say for an instance I got into a fight with somebody at school. Or one of my teachers made me feel stupid. Or somebody laughed at me for looking like a boy and swinging a bat like a boy and climbing trees like a boy in stead of acting like a girl in a pink dress and all of that. Well, when any of that kinda mess happened to me—sometimes it would happen a lot—I would go into the woods and talk to my daddy and he would tell me it was all right. He knew I was a girl, and he didn't care if I didn't wanna put on a dress or if I played baseball. He liked it. And sometimes I would go out there and I would just cry and say, "Daddy, what's happening to me? Why do they treat me like they do? There's nothing wrong with the way I'm acting, is there?"

It felt like he would be listening. Everything would be okay after that. It didn't matter anymore if people were laughing at me on the way home from school. I would go into the house and be whistling and happy and fixing myself something to eat, and Mama would come home from work tired, and look at me and say, "Girl, where you get all that spring in your step? You so spry you can get on them dishes, and then get to that kitchen floor."

Then she would look me dead in the eye and say something like, "You walking around here like you been talking to your daddy. Well, next time you do, you tell him to send home some money, you hear? And tell him not to love up other women like he does. And tell him when he left me with three children they were his children, too. I know he thinks I'm ugly, not like his women friends he meets on the road. But you tell your daddy he's the kind of ugly the Lord don't like. Now, get on them dishes, Hassalia, before I beat your behind so bad you won't be able to *say* Daddy good."

*

Esther lived with us. Her and Beetsy. They always did. Esther was married to Sting Ray, but it was peculiar, her calling herself married to him, since he was there sometimes, and then not there for a while. Everybody knew Esther was married and everybody said so. But Sting Ray wasn't what anybody talked about *to* Esther. Except when he was there, which you could never be sure for how long. When he *was* there, you couldn't talk about anything else.

First off, Sting Ray was big. Jim was pretty big, too, but he was sorta wide. He wasn't fat, but he was kinda heavy in through the middle. And he didn't move any faster than he wanted to, which was usually kinda slow. Jim could make you afraid. He moved so slow you didn't know what he was gonna do. Sting Ray was bigger, over six feet. And he had muscles. Packed muscles. He used to play football in school, when he went to school, but that wasn't the only place he got his muscles. He come up hard from a boy—worked hard—and that's how he got so strong. Like a bull.

He was quick, too. You couldn't catch him at what he was doing 'til it was too late. Sting Ray could pull out a jackknife and open it and get his arm around your neck and the knife at your throat before you knew good you made him mad. One time, Jim was standing next to his truck and this foot-high barrel of nails worked loose from where Jim had it tied, and it was fixing to fall on Jim. It woulda killed him, sure. Sting Ray happened to be working for Jim that month, or those few weeks (you never knew how long Sting Ray was gonna be around), and he was standing a couple feet from Jim. He saw he didn't have time to push Jim aside. The barrel might have landed on both of them. So he leaped up in the air and got his arms under that barrel while it was coming down—cupped it next to his chest like a football and landed on both feet. Then he just set it down.

✳

Esther was eleven years older than me. She was two years older than Johnnie. The two of 'em were kinda tight from when they were little. After I came along Johnnie was running around with his friends and starting to think he was

34

so cute, and he didn't have a lot of time any more for Esther. So, the way Mama told me later, that was when Esther kinda started looking at boys. She liked to tease a lot, but the only one she ever *really* got next to—or got next to her—was Sting Ray.

Sting Ray had people from down in Georgia, and they moved up to Chicago a little while after he was born. He had some country in him, and a lot of city, too. Crawley was kinda slow for him, I guess. We'd see him. Then he'd go away. Then come back. But it was safe, too, which some of the time had to be why we saw him when we did. Sting Ray was into one mess or another all the time, and that was one reason he'd show up in Crawley all loving up next to Esther. And Esther took him in and wrapped herself around him like a fool anytime he showed up with that grin of his and those big arms and all his talk about what he was up to, dressed in you could never tell what, driving you could never tell what, talking about you could never tell what. "Hey, baby, I'm home" was all he had to say for Esther to start falling all over him.

The whole reason Sting Ray and Esther got together wasn't any thing but a joke anyway. See, with Esther, you couldn't play like she knew what you were talking about. Because she didn't. Trying to sound evil, when the truth was she was confused. She couldn't really be evil or do evil. Which was why she stayed with Mama and was still with Mama. Mama always said to her, "Girl, you don't have to move outta this house if you don't want to."

Esther just left the thing like that. Because underneath all of that you could tell Mama was saying, "Esther, I know you're scared."

Mama never said Esther was simple. But she was. Esther couldn't *think*. That's how I knew pretty soon after I got up some size that Mama wasn't about to make Esther go anywhere. Esther could stay in that house as long as she wanted to. And, looking back, I don't think there was any way of protecting Esther.

Esther was in God's hands. I can say that now. There were hands being laid on Esther and on Beetsy. You can say God's got a plan, but I couldn't see any plan for Esther then. Then. God makes the weak and the strong and puts 'em both together. You can't tell for sure which one is which. What I've got to do now is get ready to meet whatever's waiting for me on the other side. We make plans, but we can't see the plan.

Sometimes I think Esther in her funny way knew that, knew better than the rest of us, who thought we knew and said we knew and tried to warn Esther. It seemed like she held on to Sting Ray when anybody in their right mind woulda let him go.

Esther was pretty. People used to forget. Esther had the kinda look that snuck up on people and took 'em a little while to grab hold to. When you first looked at her she didn't look like much. For one thing, she was on the heavy side in through the hips, like Mama. (Me and Johnnie were skinny, like Daddy.) Anyway, a lot of men are s'posed to like women heavy, if you feel like believing 'em. Sting Ray said he did. But men wanted a woman looking like outta *Ebony* or *Jet*, too, if they could get her, and Esther didn't look like that. She had a round face, full lips, bright brown eyes, and a smile that would make you forget what was on your mind. Esther was loud—too loud—and real friendly.

As soon as she stopped going to school—Mama decided she just wasn't getting it and let her drop out—she started doing day work with Mama. Mama said Esther didn't need to stay in school, where there was nothing but white folks laughing at her 'cause she couldn't keep up. When her teachers would talk to Mama they sounded like if the truth were to be told they didn't know what to do with Esther. Mama said she didn't want white folks making fun of her, and Esther might as well come on home and go out and do day work with her. After I got up some size and thought I was smart, when I would bring my books home from school I would show 'em to Esther—geography, biology, whatever I thought I liked that week. Esther would listen to me talking, like I was saying something important. Then all of a sudden she would just turn to me and say something like, "Has, when's Jim getting home? We don't have him something to eat when he gets here, you know how he gets. We better get up from here and cook something." But I couldn't let her cook—not by herself. I could let her snap beans, say, but not peel potatoes, 'cause she'd cut herself. I could let her check on something in the oven, but I couldn't let her take it out, 'cause she'd drop it. Esther just wasn't *steady*.

She could clean the white folks' houses with Mama, but Mama had to be right with her, or she might hurt herself. She knew how to move heavy things, like a table, but Mama couldn't let her touch china or glasses, or pretty little things the white ladies had on their dressing tables. Esther would drop that kinda stuff in a minute. She couldn't see it and hold it at the same time. It was like it dazzled her eyes. So Mama kept her mopping floors and cleaning tubs and toilets and washing windows and emptying trash, where if she dropped something it didn't matter.

Esther had long, pretty fingers. And when she would put on nail polish—I would help her, even if I didn't like that stuff myself—it would look good. And she could put on lipstick and get her hair done and look like something. When I was little, Esther would take me by the hand and we'd go down to Talbot's and buy some candy, or, even better, go down to Prince's Castle for hamburgers when whichever white lady Esther was working for that day would give her some extra money. And we'd come home and open up the bag with these hot, hot hamburgers inside, and when you'd take off the paper and open up the hamburgers the steam would come off and you could smell the hot pickles and the catsup and the chopped onion. And since she never really had that much money, we'd usually share a large chocolate malt. We'd pour the malt into a couple of cereal bowls and eat at the kitchen table.

Ma Rhetta would be upstairs sleeping or down the street at a neighbor lady's visiting, and Mama would be late coming from work, and Jim wouldn't be home yet from off the truck. So me and Esther would have the house to ourselves. We knew that when one of them got home they'd smell the hamburgers in the air and they'd know what we did, even if we weren't s'posed to, even if me and Esther could barely get it together out of her little bit of extra and my pitiful little 50-cents-a-week allowance, which I had to *work* for. Me and Esther always acted like eating those hamburgers and that malted milk was our big secret. When the folks got home, we would grin at each other and then burst out laughing. And Ma Rhetta and Mama and Jim musta known what we did, but do you know they never said a word about it?

There were times I know we didn't have the money for that. Mama would come home and make neck bones and navy beans—corn bread and a glass of water with it in the wintertime, Kool-Aid in the summer—and me and Esther would eat it and run out in the street and go jump rope with somebody or I'd play some jacks (which Esther couldn't do). Johnnie found him some ol' piece of bicycle to ride from off the truck. And Jim would find a couple a little half-broke dolls to give to me or to Esther. And we would eat those neck bones and beans and Johnnie would be teasing us after a while when all three of us would start to farting from those beans. And Johnnie would sing this silly little song: "Beans, beans, the miserable fruit / the more you eat, the more you toot"—me and Esther used to fall out laughing, and tooting; Johnnie would, too; then he'd finish it up—"the more you toot, the better you feel / let's have beans for every meal." We'd laugh, the three of us. Me not but five, Johnnie was 14 and Esther was 16. Then when Johnnie got bigger he didn't have time for me and Esther. When Esther got some more size on her she finally stopped jumping rope and met Sting Ray, and she didn't have a mind for much of anything else after that.

*

Esther. "Hassalia, Sting Ray got him a gun. And I don't mess with Sting Ray when he got bid'ness. I don't know who he do what all he do with. How I'm s'posed to? He ain't s'posed to be telling me no way, not if he got good sense. See, Hassalia, Sting Ray work a lot out of town. You can't be all up in his face. I learnt that real quick. He went up 'side my head to keep me out his bid'ness.

"Sting Ray been like that from when I first know him. Brought his good-looking Georgia self on to me when I didn't know nothing about men no kinda way. He was my first man. When you know a man that way, Hassalia, and he gets up next to you and feels on you and tells you you looking fine, a man gets holt to you and what you gonna do?

"Didn't take any time. Told me the first thing he thought about when he saw me was how he was gonna get next to me. He told me that later on. He said the first thing he thought was: 'How am I gon' get next to this woman here?' Me, when I first saw him I didn't think nothing but how big and fine he was, with that pretty little moustache he had on him.

"The first time he came talking to me, it was John Ivy and Vernon Jackson and some of them from out at the cement plant brought him by here to see Jim. It was one Sat'dy. I was just sitting doing nothing around the house. Ma Rhetta was nowhere around, Mama neither. Sting Ray and Jim and the rest of 'em were down in the basement with the radio on real loud listening to some ol' ball game, I don't know what it was. Jim done cracked open some beer 'mongst 'em, and they're laughing and talking and carrying on. I wasn't paying 'em much mind. Next thing I know, ball game over, radio off, and I hear cards slapping on this table Jim set up down there, playing 'em some fast games of tonk.

"So, I'm sitting here in the kitchen minding my own bid'ness when up came this pretty Negro from the stairs and said, 'Oh', the minute he saw me, like I was a June bug flew up in his face. And I said, 'Oh', right back at him. And he said, 'I'm downstairs with Jim and them and he told me to come up here and go into the icebox and bring us down some beer.'

"Now, that was just a lie dreamed up 'mongst the bunch of 'em down there to see how much a fool I was gon' be. Sting Ray told me later.

"I didn't know but to tell him to go on in the icebox and get what he came after. I was steady looking to see who was this ol' good-looking dark man who came up from down in the basement, from down in Georgia. Anyway, he came on in the kitchen and over to the icebox and started taking out beer and putting it on the table, next to where I was sitting. And he said, 'Mighty nice-looking Kelvinator you got yourselves here,' like he was paying more attention to the icebox than to me. It was just our ol' Kelvinator Jim found, wasn't what you call new even back then, but it did look kinda nice sitting there, so I up and said, 'Yeah, it'll keep more than beer cold.' I let him think along, honey. I was trying to tell him I got me a cold heart, too, for some sweet-talking man come up outta my basement and go to pulling beer outta my Kelvinator talking to the icebox like it was the woman and the woman like she was the icebox. I was gon' show him with his big pretty-teeth self, grinning in my face.

"See, I didn't know what was going on. Jim and the rest

of 'em down there knew I was up there by myself, and they went to betting with Sting Ray over those cards, him sitting there talking like he can get any woman he wants. So, 'stead of playing for the money he was owing them right then—it was just nickel-a-card tonk—they said to him, 'Instead of paying us this 75 cents you owe us, we'll forget the whole thing if you go upstairs and talk to Esther and see if you can get next to her, you so slick.' Well, you don't dare Sting Ray but once. He went to talking about double or nothing. So, they said, 'All right, you got a dollar-and-a-half in your pocket from every one of us as soon as you come down here and tell us you and Esther are going out somewhere tonight, and we do mean *tonight*.' Well, it *was* Sat'dy, and it was kinda natural for him to be looking for something to do, even if it wasn't but to carry somebody out to one of those roadhouses 'cross the city line, where he could buy her some whiskey.

"So, Sting Ray told 'em—this is what he told me later—'All right, I'll do like you say. I'll go on upstairs and talk to the woman, and if she says she'll go with me tonight I want a dollar-and-a-half from each and every one of you, and 50 cents more from you, John Ivy, with your big mouth, since you're the one with the widest grin on your face right now thinking I can't do it. So, that gives me five dollars to put with what I already got to sport a bit with Miss Esther this evening. Now, what y'all say?'

"Well, they went to figuring and chuckling 'mongst themselves real comical like—oh, they just couldn't stop laughing, Sting Ray told me—and finally they said to him, 'Okay, go on up there, boy, and see what you can do for yourself.' So, they made up this lie about coming to get some beer. And I told him how cold I could be, too. He was a devilish thing, the way he was looking at me.

"Next thing I knew, he was sitting down at the table opening up a bottle of beer and drinking it. I just sat there and didn't say anything, watching him drink. He spilled a little down his chin and went to wipe it with his sleeve, and he said, 'Lord, look at me making a mess here this afternoon. With something this pretty 'cross the way from me it's no wonder I do, no wonder at all.' Oh, Sting Ray can talk him some real foolish talk when he wants to, honey.

"I just looked at him and said, 'Well, if you were downstairs 'cross the table from your card partner you prob'ly wouldn't be spilling beer on yourself, 'cause you must be right, whoever he is, he isn't near 'bout pretty as me.' I wasn't gon' jump up and down 'cause some sweaty-smelling man came in from a hard afternoon working on a truck and started talking sweet to somebody he saw sitting there when he came up into the kitchen to get some beer. Like I was the beer and he could open me with an opener, too. Unh-unh, honey.

"So, we sat there. And I said to him, 'Don't you think those men downstairs are gon' be wanting that beer so y'all can go on with your card game, or whatever you're doing down there?' He said, 'I'm not gon' take those men nothing 'til I'm through talking to you. They can come up here and get this beer themself if they want it that bad.' And I said, 'Well, I don't know what you got to say to me, but I don't see why anybody's beer needs to get warm waiting for it.' And he said, 'Well, I won't let it get warm, then. Tell you what. Let me take you out to the Crow's Corner tonight out on the highway and we'll drink us some beer and a little whiskey, too, you and me, and do us a little dancing. How that sound to you?'

"I said, 'Scuse me, but I don't think I heard your name.' He went to laughing and said, 'You could have just as good a time if you didn't know my name. It's Ray. Nobody calls me anything but Sting Ray, though.'

"I said, 'Sting Ray? I never heard such.' And he said, 'It's from underneath the ocean. It'll sting you quick and kill you dead if you get down there with it where you ain't s'posed to be.' He was still smiling. I said, 'Well, Mr. Sting Ray from the bottom of the ocean, looks to me like you didn't come from nowhere farther down than the basement here this afternoon. I guess I will go on out to the Crow with you tonight. And if I get stung you can just answer for it to my Mama and my Uncle Jim downstairs.'

"Truth was, Hassalia, I did get stung by Sting Ray that night. He was around here working for Jim and staying over in Mrs. Crandall's basement with some of the rest of those men from down in Georgia. Then after a couple a weeks he went away. I don't know where.

"When he came back six months later, what was I doing but carrying Beetsy, who he left me with, but he didn't know that. So, we got married. And Mama said he could stay here, and that was all right with Jim, too. I was real happy. Remember, Has? But, see, this much I do know—we may can get us a baby, but it's a lot harder to get a daddy, do you know that one thing? It's easier to get a daddy than keep one, the way Ma Rhetta used to say.

"Anyway, Sting Ray wasn't here when Beetsy was born. He told me later he wanted to be, Has, but he had some bid'ness to take care of. He says he can't do the bid'ness he does in Crawley. Sting Ray's smart, Hassalia. He says he's gon' give up all of his traveling around, and him and me and Beetsy are gon' go somewhere and get us a house of our own.

"Mama's got her little Beetsy baby to wait with her for Daddy to come home, don't I, sugar? And don't Mama's baby love her daddy? Yes, she does. I know you do, sugar.

"See, that's why I'm telling you, Hassalia, when Sting Ray's nervous like he is now, nobody needs to be on him with a whole lot of questions. I know he's got a gun. And I'm not worrying about no gun, Hassalia. So you just gon' have to do some worrying about some gun by yourself. These highway patrolmen got guns, too, Sting Ray says. If the man needs protection I guess he needs protection. I'm not mixing in that.

"Sting Ray goes away, but he comes back. Must mean he's trying to do something for me and Beetsy. So, maybe I'm not s'posed to see him but so much. You go to circling around a man and holding him down, using your baby like a hammer 'cross his head, you won't do nothing but run him off. Looks to me like what Mama did with Daddy Izell was stay on him so bad 'til he felt like he couldn't come back 'cause he knows she's just gon' be on him some more about when he's coming back to *stay*. And it's not like he doesn't do for us. He sends her a little something when he's got it.

"All I know for sure is, Sting Ray's the daddy of this baby girl, here. When you get a man, Hassalia, you're gon' see what I'm talking about. Then you'll know what you've got to do to keep him. It's easier to get one than to keep him, Hassalia, like Ma Rhetta said."

PART TWO

MA RHETTA, 1953

It cost something for us to be here.

—Ntozake Shange
Spell #7

ONE NIGHT, THE SUMMER WHEN I WAS FIFTEEN, me and Ma Rhetta were sitting on the front porch. We were watching fireflies. Folks white and black out for a stroll would pass by and Ma Rhetta would say, "Good evening." But she was talking to me the whole time. Lowlike. I don't remember where Mama was, or Jim. Aunt Fanny was over and was back in the kitchen making fudge. She came out on the porch to let me lick the bowl and eat some of the pecans before she put 'em in, but she wasn't really paying any attention to what Ma Rhetta was saying to me, and after I had my lick she went back in the house and tended to her baking. Jim coulda been anywhere. I know he wasn't in the house. Esther and Beetsy musta been upstairs keeping cool. It was just me and Ma Rhetta on the porch. Through the screen door we could hear Aunt Fanny singing to herself in the kitchen.

Ma Rhetta. "You got to watch out for how a man gon' do you, Hassalia. I know you don't wanna be thinkin' 'bout no mens yet. I see you runnin' outta here playin' basketball and everything else wit' these boys from over to the high school, the white ones and the colored ones. And yo' Mama and me neither one worryin' 'bout it. We know you ain't got no feelin' that's out the way for any o' these here boys. They treatin' you like you one of 'em, and long as you can run fast and jump high as they do they gon' go on doin' that. Yo'

Mama don't see the harm to it, and I don't neither. Lef' up to me you would put on a dress and start actin' like a young lady 'round here. But the time for that gon' come. Some o' these lowlife niggers lookin' up yo' dress, it ain't no wonder you don't wanna put none on. These white boys, most of 'em not too far from gettin' off they bicycles and thinkin' 'bout gettin' into they first automobiles. They got any sense they not gon' be triflin' wit' no colored girl. They daddies don't buy no automobile for no boy be triflin' wit' no colored girl.

"But don't you stay out late wit' these white boys, Hassalia. Don't act no fool. Don't you get off alone in the woods wit' 'em neither. You too big for that now. These youngsters got feelin's they don't know 'bout that can sneak up on 'em. And they be sneakin' up on you, too, before you know it, Hassalia. So, you look to yo'self, girl, rippin' and runnin' wit' these boys out here. They don't *want* no colored girl, but they don't truthfully know what they want. Don't let me catch you runnin' after 'em, Hassalia. Don't be no white boy's somethin' easy.

"But you gon' get you a feelin' for a man one o' these days, Hassalia. And there ain't gon' be nowhere to hide. I started early, Hassalia, and I know. I wasn't but a chile o' fifteen, like you are now, when a man looked the wrong way at me. Or was it the right way?

"See, Hassalia, it was like this here: my Mama, yo' greatgrandmama, was a po' woman worked for white folks down in Memphis. Her daddy, my granddaddy, was a horse handler workin' 'round the stables and such. He didn't have no time for him no wife and chil'ren, so Mama was raised on up by *her* Mama for a time, then wit' her Auntie Belle, then back to her mama, and on like that. So, she come up as a girl takin' work on. She met my daddy one day when she downtown wit' her white lady and this man wit' his horse cart was there sellin' fruit from off the little ol' farm

48

he had not far from there. And he was so happy when his eyes lit on Mama that he got boastful enough in himself to follow her and her white lady home. Careful like. But that's how he found out where she lived. Well, he went to courtin' and it came time for them to go on and get married.

"But Mama wasn't no farm woman. It just weren't in her to work in a house alone all day doin' that tendin', wit' nobody for miles to talk to, and just wait for her man to come in out the fields. This man who was her husband I call my daddy, Hassalia, 'cause for the longest time she called him that to me. But he wasn't my daddy. Another man was my daddy, and he was yo' real greatgranddaddy—a man Mama come on one Sunday she and her husband went to church. This man promised Mama he would carry her away wit' him. But he lef' 'way from there, and she find out she carryin' his chile. She know it's hisn 'cause her and her husband ain't been together for a long time.

"All she can think about is how she gon' get outta there. She know her husband ain't gon' be takin' to another man's chile. It just ain't in his nature. She go back to Memphis and find her some work wit' some white folks, and Lord bless the cook in the white lady's house, she let my Mama stay wit' her when my Mama birth me. Mama was alone in the world. Didn't have no husband, and didn't know where to find my real daddy. All she had was me. See, Hassalia, a man get you when you ain't lookin' and when you ain't feelin' at yo'self. I wasn't nothin' but a chile o' fifteen, and along come this slick-haired man wit' pretty teeth and yellow shoes and I ain't never seen nobody like him before. Mama kept an eye, like they say, but I slipped away from her one Sunday and met this man out at an old carnival place that was rotted out 'cause it ain't been used for a long while. The place was filled up wit' water and there was snakes all 'round. Never will forget. I was wearin' my onliest pair o' good shoes and took 'em off and tied 'em 'round my neck, and took off my stockin's and was walkin' barefoot out to this ol' rundown carnival place where this man tol' me he was gonna be. I don't know what kinda fool I was. Didn't have nobody wit' me. He coulda been out there wit' a bunch o' other mens and brought me to Lord knows what kinda harm. But I went on ahead, thinkin' in my mind this man was just somebody who was gon' be good to me.

"I know I was happy out there under my straw hat wit' that dust between my toes and holdin' up my skirt to try to keep it from gettin' tangled in the cockleburrs 'long side the road. I was hummin' and singin' and, I can't tell you why, Hassalia, but I didn't feel like no harm was gon' come to me. It was like I was s'posed to meet this man out there. And after I did I would be a woman. I didn't know all what was s'posed to happen. I thought I just had to be alone wit' a man out in the sun next to the water, watchin' for the snakes and keepin' my hat on to keep the hot sun off.

"Turned out he was a drummer, sold to colored from town to town, ladies' hats and ribbons and lace handker-chiefs and all kind o' pretty things like that. First time I was ever near a man smelled so good. He smelled like a flower patch. And wore a pomade made his hair sparkle in that sunshine. We finds us a old log out there next to this swampy place—he poked under it and inside to make sure they wasn't no snakes—and he lays out a kerchief for me to sit on, and another one for him. He takes off his hat.

"And somethin' happened, Hassalia, soon as we sat down. This man treated me like I didn't belong to my Mama. He talked respectful 'bout her, but like I had my own lookout for myself. I *didn't*. But he acted like I coulda just got on up any time and walked on away from him, like I was stayin' there wit' him, was out there meetin' him, just 'cause I wanted. And I was there 'cause I thought he wanted me there. Or, that's what I tol' myself. But, see, he was right. I wanted to. I wanted to be somewhere Mama couldn't see, doin' somethin' she couldn't see, turnin' into somebody she wasn't ever gonna know. So, when he went to put his hands on me all I could think was, 'Mama's not here. Mama's not watchin' me do this. I'm gon' be somebody Mama don't know nothin' 'bout.' And he broke me.

"I didn't let him walk me but so far back into town. I never saw him again. After a while, I didn't even want to. I was different. I think Mama mighta known I was different. But she didn't say nothin'. I got it in my head, Hassalia, that I had to get me a man to get away from her. Like there wasn't no other way. We was livin' in wit' these white folks, and we didn't have nothin'. Times got hard, Mama used to let me go out in the country and pick, so me and her would have us a little somethin'. The white folks give us a roof over our head, but not much else to speak of. White lady would not give us nothin' she th'owed out. We had to slip and take it. She might see to it it got to po' white folks, but not to us there in her house. Not if it was lef' up to her, we wouldna had it. So if me and Mama needed somethin'—a dress, a pair o' shoes besides what we worked in, somethin' nice we wanted to put in our room that didn't belong to the white lady—we had to find the money for it the best way we could.

"So, I would go out and pick. Mama wasn't old, but she was too old to be out in the hot sun pickin' apples or berries. The worst was pickin' tobacco. Hot? Chile. Break yo' back to make half a dollar. My hands got so rough from the pickin' for a while there my white folks couldn't let me serve dinner or take care o' the chil'ren. So it got to where I wasn't doin' nothin' but scrubbin' and cleanin' and stayin' on my hands and knees. Between white folks and Negro mens, let me tell you, Hassalia, they will keep you on yo' knees."

Aunt Fanny came out on the porch with a plate full of fudge and a pitcher of cold lemonade. Ma Rhetta took a piece. I took two. We both had lemonade. Ma Rhetta bit on her piece of fudge and just let it sit in her mouth. I knew she wasn't through talking to me. So I chewed on my first piece of fudge, taking my time on those pecans, and let the second piece sit on the paper napkin Aunt Fanny brought me. I knew Ma Rhetta was waiting for Aunt Fanny to go on back in the house. I felt funny, but I knew Ma Rhetta was talking to me like I was gonna be a woman, even though I wasn't one yet and wasn't sure when I was gonna get to be one and if I did what I was gon' do then.

And I could tell right then Ma Rhetta didn't ever talk to Aunt Fanny the way she was talking to me right then, even if Aunt Fanny was already a woman, s'posedly. And I knew Ma Rhetta never would talk to Aunt Fanny like that. It wasn't that Aunt Fanny was a girl. She wasn't. I was. But Aunt Fanny wasn't a woman in her own mind. That soldier didn't finish in her mind. He didn't make her a woman *there*. He made her afraid to be a woman. Being with a man didn't make you a woman, you had to be with him a certain way, was what Ma Rhetta was trying to tell me. Or would finish trying to tell me as soon as Aunt Fanny went back in the house to clean up the kitchen before she went on back to Uncle Grease's house.

But it was real nice there for a few minutes. Just the three of us. I didn't think about it at the time—I was too busy wanting Ma Rhetta to get back to her story—but Aunt Fanny was doing a lot that night. The three of us sat there eating fudge and drinking lemonade, and after me and Ma Rhetta told Aunt Fanny how good the first bite was, didn't any of us say another word for the nicest little while. The fireflies kept going on and off. And 'cross the way Mr. Jarvis came out and put on his sprinkler. Now and again a car would go by real slow. It was too hot a night to do anything fast. The fudge was melting in my mouth and sticking to my fingers and I knew I wouldn't be able to clean it all off until I went back in the house, and I wasn't gonna do that 'til Ma Rhetta was through talking. Aunt Fanny sat there eating fudge and looking glad me and Ma Rhetta were there eating it with her. She was the woman she *could* be, sitting there in the summer dark on the porch of a house she hated, next to her mother, who she musta thought hated *her*, even if Fanny couldn't figure why, and next to me, her niece, who, even acting like a boy, was already getting closer to being a woman the way Fanny thought a woman was s'posed to be.

Aunt Fanny came back to the house that night just to visit. And on a dare to herself she decided to go into the kitchen and stir up something sweet. Hunted up the cocoa and the powdered sugar and the pecans and the butter and the vanilla extract, and made something sugar dark and crunchy that was melting right into the night, right into her and me and Ma Rhetta.

Without a word, she picked up the plate of fudge and the half-empty pitcher of lemonade and took it all back in the kitchen. I guess she cleaned up and went on home out the back door, because me and Ma Rhetta didn't see her for the rest of the night.

But what if by the time she brought out the fudge she was *already* finished cleaning up in the kitchen? Maybe after she left the plate of fudge on the counter in the kitchen and put the half-empty pitcher back in the refrigerator she crept back quiet as a cat into the living room and, without me or Ma Rhetta hearing a sound, took a seat there right next to the screen door, where she could hear Ma Rhetta in the swing, talking, and me on the railing, breathing. Maybe she heard every word Ma Rhetta said. Maybe her womanhood was a question to her, too, that she wanted the answer to. Maybe she knew that was what me and Ma Rhetta had to be talking about, because colored women alone without men on hot summer nights are always talking about that, even when they're talking about the church choir, or what to do for the baby's croup, or which butcher at the A&P gives the best ham hocks. Maybe colored women are always talking about what's being done to 'em by colored men, and why colored men do it. And maybe that white soldier was one way Aunt Fanny thought she'd be able to stop asking those questions. But here they were back again, 'cause that white man wasn't an answer. He was another question about colored men.

So maybe, just maybe, Aunt Fanny wasn't out of her mind at all. Maybe after what happened with that soldier she moved into another part of it, and was watching us and listening to us all from there, like a princess in a castle in a fairy tale, listening that night from right inside the house to Ma Rhetta talking and me listening, knowing Ma Rhetta would think she wouldn't dare, 'cause s'posedly all those questions about men were already over and answered for her.

Maybe Aunt Fanny never lost her mind at all, but was, like every colored woman in the world, still looking for it. And maybe she found a piece of it that night listening to Ma Rhetta. Or maybe she lost hold of another piece of it. And slipped out the back door and went careful, quiet, through all of Jim's junk, back to Uncle Grease's house, back into the part of her mind where the white soldier wasn't finished with her yet. Maybe.

Ma Rhetta. "Hezekiah was yo' Mama's Daddy, Hassalia. He yo' granddaddy. He was a conjure man. I don't know what kind o' sense I thought I had when I ups and chases this man. Had no notion he would give me no baby. I didn't have that feelin' for him first time I come up on him.

"See, back in them times, Hassalia, colored man move, didn't hardly nobody notice. Roamin' 'round little town to little town. Jump off into a city like Memphis, then go back to the little bit o' places for a while. Some colored was goin' out West, clear to California. Some was headin' north— New York, Chicago, Detroit.

"Hezekiah was one o' the ones come through Memphis

goin' Lord knew where. Mama was a Christian. Didn't take
to no foolishness 'bout roots and herbs and bones and
conjurin'. Said that was old-timey and colored folks wit'
good sense didn't cotton to it. So I didn't neither. I wasn't
studyin' no conjurin' when this little man come through
wit' his magic dust and big purple and white bandannas and
wide-brimmed hats and fast-talkin' ways. You wouldna
known he was no conjure man to look at him. Not straight
off. True, he wore these black hats wit' the big soft brim, and
he kep' a red feather in the band. But he didn't dress no
otherways peculiar, didn't have to. Not 'lessen you want to
count the rings he had on his fingers, one of 'em gold and
the other one silver. The gold one had a red ruby in it he
could shine into folks' eyes and carry 'em off clean out they
mind, like they was a baby didn't know what to do 'cept
what Hezekiah tell 'em. But that ain't the way he got next
to me. I was 18 the summer he come through Memphis. A
couple o' other mens trifled wit' me since that drummer, but
not for no time to speak of. Tol' myself I was lookin' for a
man wit' some get up, and I didn't see none in the niggers
'round there. They was po', married or shif'less. Seemed like
the good-lookin' ones come to church was already took by
the time they come to the Lord, and soon as you see one you
see his wife and little baby right next to him. Or else they
was no count at all, gamblin' and livin' fast and doin' Lord
knew what all, and I was still wit' Mama and the white folks,
and they wouldna stood for none o' that. The little bit o'
foolin' wit mens I done, I slipped and done. Mama was
gettin' mo' and mo' po'ly, bones gettin' mo' crippled up and
hurtful every year.

"That's how I come on ol' Hezekiah. This friend o' mine,
May Ella, was a simple fool worked near 'bout where I did.
And I was tellin' her one day 'bout Mama and her pains, and
she tol' me 'bout this man done come into town and held
him a meetin' the other evenin' in somebody's house wit' a

whole lot o' folks. And some of 'em was feelin' po'ly. He raised one lady up and caused her to talk. Loosed another one from a bad ol' grip 'bout the head brung her nothin' but headaches all the time. Another one who was bleedin' that very evenin', he took loose her bandages where she done stanched the cut and he stopped the blood right then and there. May Ella said she saw him do it. I said, 'Girl, get on 'way from me. How you know them folks ain't fixed it all up wit' him befo' the meetin'? You know the peoples yo'self?' She say, 'Rhett, girl, I'm tellin' you 'twasn't like that. No, I didn't know the folks. But crippled up like the one woman was, she couldna been foolin'. And I *saw* the woman bleedin' from her arm, and this Hezekiah got to talkin' over this woman's arm and holdin' her hand and callin' on spirits, I'm tellin' you chile, the bleedin' just *stopped*. Saw the girl the other day and she say her arm all but healed, ain't nothin' there now but a little bit o' scar. Just that quick. Doctor tol' her it was gonna take *weeks* to get right. She right in three, four *days*. I'm tellin' you, yo' Mama need to see what this man can do for her.'

"Well, I'm still not studyin' this man. And I ain't thinkin' o' tellin' Mama not one thing 'bout no conjure man wit' no tricks. Shoot.

"The next day I looks out the white folks' window and here's this man up in the back yard, sittin' there wit' his eyes closed, mumblin'. The white folks done got out early that mornin', thank the Lord, and took Mama wit' 'em to tote. The butler was drivin' the coach, so wasn't nobody but me and some o' the stable hands near 'bout.

"But I says to myself, If I don't get this mumblin' nigger out these folks' back yard me and Mama gon' be lookin' for another place. I knew who he was from what May Ella tol' me. I didn't intend to trifle wit' trash. I went out there wavin' my broom. I said, 'You, you ol' conjure man wit' yo' foolishness. I know who you are. And I know May Ella done sent you. Her and the Devil. You ain't 'bout to get not a nickel out o' my Mama wit' yo' conjure tricks—takin' po' folks' money and fillin' 'em up wit' believin' you gon' ease they misery. Get on 'way from here, nigger, 'fo I call the stable hands and get you run off from this place, and then I'ma call some policemens and get you run 'way from 'round here but good. Git!'

"Well, I'm just hollerin' and wavin' my broom and carryin' on, thinkin' I'm gon' get him 'way from there by puttin' the fear o' white folks' policemens in him. Honey, I didn't know what this man had ready for me.

"He open his eyes slowlike and stop chantin' whatever it was he was sayin' to himself and loosened up his body—he was standin' froze still at first—and he look at me. He say, 'Miz Rhetta, ma'm, I heard what you said. And you can call whoever you want to call to come and chase me away. But I didn't come here to take care o' yo' Mama. You the one ailin'. Badder than you know.'

"I looks him up and down and I says, 'I'm feelin' strong enough to break this broom 'cross yo' nappy head.' He don't say nothin'. I said, 'Mr. Man, I'm 'bout to call these hands from out the stable and they bring the dogs and run you off from here.' He say, 'Woman wit' a shriveled up heart would do what you say you gon' do. You can run me 'way from here if you want. But what about the dogs chasin' you 'round and 'round in yo' mind, tearin' at yo' dreams just like they be tearin' at my flesh in a minute here, soon as you call 'em ? I mean the dogs in yo' dreams causin' you to sweat and holler and run for yo' life so you don't lose yo' mind, just like you gon' have me runnin' in a minute here?' I say, 'Mr. Man, I ain't got nothin' chasin' me nowhere, and I'm gon' set them dogs on you this minute.' He don't even listen to me. He say, 'Ma'm, you grievin' for yo' own self, and you ain't even dead yet.'

"I jumped back. He reached right into me that time. It

seemed like me and Mama would never get outta them folks' house and have nothin' o' our own. And they wasn't no man comin' for either one o' us, it looked like for sure. If Mama was to die, what would I do but bury her and keep on the same way? If them white folks wouldn't still have me, I'd have to find me some mo'. I didn't have nobody, Hassalia, just Mama, and she was gettin' weaker every day.

"But, like the man said, I was the one sick, sicker than her, 'cause I didn't have what folks used to call a way north. That was just a way colored folks had o' talkin'. 'Keep you a way north, honey, if you can.' They wasn't talkin' 'bout comin' north for real and for true. They mean: try to have somethin' set by if you have to leave where you at. When you said somebody 'didn't have no way north' you was sayin' they was so po' they wasn't gon' get out o' bein' beholdin' to white folks the rest o' they days.

"So, this man wit' his talk got right up next to me. I thought he was from the Devil right then, but I knew he done spoke the truth, too, and he cut me hard when he did. Finally I say, 'What you want wit' me?' And he say, 'To give you the healin' in my hands, sister, the healin' in my hands.' You can say he put a spell on me if you want to, Hassalia. I think he did. But I didn't believe in no spells or none o' that. So I don't know how he did it, to this day. He didn't do no mo' chantin'. He mumbled, but it was just the mumblin' a man do when he havin' his way wit' a woman. She strugglin' and her strugglin' ain't doin' her no good, 'cause she don't rightly know is she strugglin' to hold on or let go. So, she cease to strugglin'. He had his way wit' me, right there in them folks' kitchen on that hot, hot mornin'.

"He took off his hat and laid his hands right 'cross my heart, and next thing I knew he laid me right down on that cool kitchen floor, flies buzzin' over my head in my bowl of hoecake batter. You could say he had him some kinda magic in his hands, 'cause soon as he touched me what I was feelin' went all the way through me, into my heart and down between my legs and on out the bottom o' my feet. He had me unexpected, like them flies was havin' that hoecake batter. They wasn't s'posed to, but they was. They had it and had it and had it, 'cause they wasn't nobody to stop 'em."

I wasn't thinking it back then, but I think about it now: Was Aunt Fanny there in the living room, listening to all Ma Rhetta was saying? Was she remembering what it was like with her and the soldier? Nobody stopped them either. The soldier stopped. What made him stop? What made him start?

Ma Rhetta. "I started slippin' out to him after that. It would be up in the daytime. He was stayin' at a colored boardin' house not too far from the house. Mama and the white folks couldn't really call me out if I said it took me longer than I expected at the vegetable market, or I come 'cross somebody from church while I was runnin' out to get a basket o' blackberries for a pie. The white lady or Mama neither one think twice about it. I didn't give 'em a chance to noway. I surprised myself how slick I got. Hezekiah, he go on wit' his meetin's and his healin's in the evenin's. Mama heard tell o' him from one o' the church sisters come to visit. But she wasn't studyin' it, and I didn't say a word. Me and her never talked about him.

"Thing was, he was right about Mama. She *was* sick. She was dyin'. I knew it, but I didn't want to know. I didn't know what I was gon' do when she was gone. 'Got nothin' to pass on to you but strength and pain, Rhetta,' she would say to me, and laugh a little sad ol' laugh down in her th'oat, and go back to her sewin' basket, darnin' for the white folks. She didn't talk about me and no man, 'cause she musta been hopin' I wouldn't find none, and stay wit' her. I didn't know how to leave Mama. But just when you thinkin' 'bout how to leave somebody, they'll up and leave you. You watch and see if I'm not right, Hassalia.

"Mama died. She went fast, thank the Lord. Just didn't wake up one mornin'. I carried her on to the cemetery. White folks said I could stay, but I didn't want to, not wit' Mama gone. I didn't want to live there without her. And I was too young for them to put me over anybody. They'da put me under somebody and I couldna stood for that in that house, long as me and Mama worked there to make the place run like somethin'.

"I was scared. I got mo' scared when I found out I was carryin' yo' Mama. This was 19 and 12, Hassalia, in Memphis, *Tenn*essee. A colored girl lookin' for work and carryin' her a baby was in a world o' trouble.

"At first Hezekiah didn't believe me. Then he said he didn't believe it was hisn. I said he knew it was. He say, 'Woman, a man o' the spirit got no time for no babies. I go where I'm moved. Where the healin' need takes me . You and yo' baby lookin' for a daddy and you think you done lighted on me. Well, ain't nobody gon' say this my baby but you. Ain't nobody even seen us together.'

"I'm standin' there in this man's roomin' house, Hassalia, and I want to scream out to the landlady and the whole world what wrong he done me, and how he 'bout to leave me wit' his chile. And he see it comin' up 'cross my face, and he say, real quick like, 'Don't try it, gal. I know what you thinkin'. You 'bout to call me out befo' this lady who's boardin' me, and you think her and the rest o' the folks gon' set the law on me. But I'm tellin' you, gal, I'll let 'em know I'm the one tryin' to heal you, not hurt you. And tell 'em you talkin' out o' yo' head 'bout me bein' the daddy o' yo' baby, when I'm the one tryin' to ease yo' mind so we can *find* the daddy. Go on and yell, gal. These folks ain't gon' believe you.'

"He was right. A whole lot o' womens wit' a whole lot wrong wit' 'em, includin' daddies that couldn't be found, was under Hezekiah's care in Memphis. They'da just thought

I was another one out o' her mind. I stood there and wouldn't cry. I didn't know what to do. I didn't know how to just leave. I didn't want to walk out o' there and let this man walk away from me and his chile like that. But I didn't know how to call him to account. I coulda kicked up a fuss wit' the church folks and they mighta got together to see to it he lef' on 'way from there.

"But Hezekiah was headin' out anyway. I said to him, 'The day you come to me in my back yard and took me on the floor o' the lady's kitchen, I said to myself you was from the Devil. I couldn't fight you and the Devil at the same time. The two o' you was too strong for me. Now I know I was right. But you and the Devil don't want y'all's chile, do you? Well, why I got to have the chile, then? You ain't gon' walk away from yo' chile, Mr. Man, 'cause little while from now there ain't gon' *be* no chile to walk away from. You and the Devil ain't carryin' this baby. I am. And you and the Devil can't have it.'

"I walked on out o' there. Hezekiah lef' Memphis the next day. Don't know whether he was scared or not. A few weeks later I got me a poker from out the lady's stable—I was still livin' there in the room me and Mama used to have together—and tried to jab up in myself and kill that Devil's baby dead. I didn't do nothin' but hurt myself.

"I sat down there and cried for three days without movin'. The white lady thought I lost my mind, and tol' me I had to get on 'way from there. May Ella had some friends who was comin' north, and they said I could ride wit' 'em to Chicago. That's where yo' Mama was born. Soon as she was, I thought about that gold ring Hezekiah used to wear. Her eyes had that sparkle that'll get you and hold you, like that Devil man's ring would. So I went on ahead and named her Ruby."

Mr. Jarvis finished sprinkling. The night got real quiet. My behind ached from sitting on the railing. We had a big, long porch swing with a cushion on it, and I got up and sat at the other end of it from Ma Rhetta. With my long legs I could fold one of 'em under me and stick the other one way out and swing that swing more than Ma Rhetta in house slippers could with her short little legs. But I didn't. I put my weight into the swing gentle and didn't stop the way Ma Rhetta was swinging at all. I put my arm 'cross the back of the swing. Inside the living room one little lamp let some light out the window. It fell on my arm and 'cross the gray in Ma Rhetta's hair. We were mostly in the dark. Keeping lights off in the summertime kept down the moths and the mosquitoes.

The way I was looking at Ma Rhetta, I was telling her to go on. I knew I couldn't *make* her go on. But she was up to my Mama being born and I wanted to hear the rest. I mean the rest about the men. Mama used to tell me about her and Uncle Jim growing up sometimes. But she wouldn't talk about no daddies. I got so I stopped asking. The daddies weren't there. I didn't know why. And maybe now Ma Rhetta was gonna tell me about the daddies. I knew Ma Rhetta had four kids, and all of 'em had different daddies. And I knew Ma Rhetta didn't marry any of 'em. But that didn't sit wrong with me 'til right then. If she wanted to tell me, I wanted to know. But *what* did I want to know? The night got even more quiet. Crickets was all. I looked at the stars. It felt like somebody turned the world off and was letting me and Ma Rhetta look. She was looking at the sky, too, but I could tell she wasn't really looking. Her eyes were shiny bright, so I didn't say anything. I just looked. The sky was so big out there. You could tell the stars, one from the other. They seemed close, like you could jump up there and run around amongst 'em. We sat there. Then she started up again.

Ma Rhetta. "She wasn't no chile o' no Devil, yo' Mama. I didn't need to be goin' all up in myself tryin' to harm her neither, like I done. Yo' Mama didn't come from the Devil, Hassalia. Don't think I'm sayin' that. That ol' Hezekiah was from the Devil. I *do* mean that. Hisn wasn't the last bit o' devilment I saw in a man. I don't know where it comes from, Hassalia, but it's there. Man or woman, the Devil finds the Devil in you."

Ma Rhetta was tellin' me the Devil was up there in the dark, too, in betwixt those stars. I couldn't see him, but he was there.

Ma Rhetta. "I had hard times in Chicago, Hassalia. It was a goodtime town for lots o' folks, includin' colored. But I didn't know which kind o' way to turn. Yo' Mama was a little bit o' baby, and me, well, I knew how to work for white folks.

"Turned out May Ella had a cousin name o' Jennie, lived there on the West Side. Jennie was a good kinda gal, seemed like. Didn't seem fast when you met her, right pretty, proper talkin' and dressed elegant. I didn't pay her all that much mind. When Jennie tol' May Ella I could knock on the door o' this white family Jennie knew 'cause they needed a maid, I thanked the Lord and went on out to see 'em.

"It was a big, pretty place on the North Side. It was a while before I met the lady o' the house, mister either. I worked under the butler and the cook, both of 'em white. There was another colored woman there, Clarice. She was the upstairs maid. She had all the beddin' and linen and bathrooms to tend to, every day, plus usin' me and the butler when she had big cleanin' jobs up there—and the driver, too, if he was idle and we had any heavy liftin' to do. I worked downstairs. I had to keep the drawin' room ready to receive callers, serve 'em, plus stay in the kitchen and help cook wit' all she had to do.

"Cook, name o' Mrs. Folsom, was a hard white woman when she was of a mind to be, and she wasn't particular 'bout colored, you could tell. Don't slip up. She'd start treatin' you like you didn't have any sense at all 'til you work back in her favor. Me and Clarice used to talk about it when we had a minute, but we didn't talk too much and I never really did know Clarice, we had so much work to do. Bein' all in somebody's face all day don't make you want to see 'em on your onliest day off, which for me was Sunday and every other Tuesday. Cook took off Sat'day, so I filled in for her that day. But there wasn't too much on a Sat'day. Folks ate simple in the mornin' and like as not would eat out for the rest o' the day. If they was gon' be in Sat'day night and holdin' a dinner party cook would work and be off another day. I worked, chile, let me tell you, for that $7 a week and carfare. Nine to nine. From cleanin' up breakfast dishes to servin' dinner. Clarice worked seven to seven, so she served breakfast, upstairs or down. We both helped wit' lunch or tea, and she helped me and cook get started on dinner. Me and butler did the servin'. Wonder was, they let me bring yo' Mama wit' me, long as she didn't make no trouble. And she was a good little baby girl, praise the Lord for her. Nice little room downstairs for her to sleep in. Cook had a boy, six, and he took to yo' Mama and kep' her comp'ny.

"So, we weren't livin' in. When I got off I had to bundle her little sleepy self up and take her home to the West Side. And wake her up in the mornin' to come wit' me to work. But she didn't mind ridin' the trolley, and I sho didn't have nobody to leave her wit'.

"The funny part of it didn't come to me 'til I was there a while. The folks were name o' Addleton, and come to find out from May Ella – she didn't tell me right off–that the Mister was keepin' comp'ny wit' Jennie. Jennie had the favor of a few white gentlemens she did for, and kep' herself real well while she was doin' it. The Mister done already tol' Jennie his wife was lookin' for a maid and asked her did she know anybody. She liked May Ella and me enough to let May Ella give me the folks' name. Jennie already told the

Mister her cousin was fresh up north from Memphis wit' a friend who worked for a good white family down there and was lookin' for a place. That's how I got the name o' the cook. Went out there and talked to her and got the place. But you'da never known to look at the Mister and Missus that anything wasn't right betwixt 'em. Had two beautiful chil'ren, and the Missus was a pretty little thing. And right pleasant to do for. I couldn't understand him and Jennie carryin' on, but I didn't know Jennie to show like she even gave it a thought. Lord knows I wasn't gon' say nothin' to nobody. I would see Jennie time by time, and I didn't say nothin'. I would talk about the place, about the Mister, even, but I didn't look at her like I knew what was goin' on between him and her, and she didn't act like I knew. She knew I had better sense than to say anything. What would ita got me? I'd lose my place, is all. And Jennie had her some colored men she was friendly wit', too, and you wouldna wanted to get on the bad side o' some o' them ruffians. Oh, they was slick enough, all right, but ruffians to the bone, yes sir.

"Was one of 'em led me to mo' trouble. See, turned out this Jennie, honey, she was a pistol. I liked Jennie. But Jennie kep' her some mess goin'. She had this fella Brown comin' 'round there doin' whatever kind o' no-good she needed done on the sly without anybody knowin'. *Mister* Brown. Had a first name, but didn't nobody ever call him by it. 'Ask Mr. Brown if he'll do that for you.' 'Go see if Mr. Brown done come in yet.' 'Mr. Brown, what horse is yo' money on today?' Like that.

"One Sunday I was home wit' Ruby. She was sick. I didn't know wit' what. She fret and fret, and I felt her and she was gettin' hotter and hotter, and I was thinkin' fever was gon' carry off my chile that very day. She didn't want to eat. I held her, I walked wit' her, I talked to her, I sat in my little room and rocked her, and she just fret, fret, fret. A cool bath helped for a little while, but directly she would go back to frettin'.

"Was it the angel o' the Lord, or what? I don't know. But right while I was sittin' there wit' my chile thinkin' I got to find a doctor and I didn't know none—right then my landlady knocked on my door and said a gentleman was callin'. Mr. Brown. I said, 'Oh, please, let him up.' I was holdin' Ruby in my arms and she was frettin', so the landlady could see I wasn't up to nothin' no good, not right then anyway. I come to find out more about her, too, later on that woulda tol' you she wouldna paid no mind no way, but I didn't know none o' that then.

"Well, Mr. Brown came up and saw me in the way I was and he said, 'Sister'—he called me Sister from the start, kinda teasin', like I was real churchified, which I *was* to his way o' thinkin'—he said, 'Sister, what's got you lookin' so?' He could see in my eyes I wasn't at myself. And I said, 'Oh, Mr. Brown, look here at my little baby girl. She's burnin' up wit' fever.' And he felt on Ruby real tender wit' the back o' his hand. And he said, 'Sister, I'm gon' go and get a doctor.' And I said, 'Well, I don't have much, but whatever he'll take from me I'll give him, and I'll pay him whatever else he needs directly, out o' my pay.' And he said, 'Don't think o' that. Just keep cool water at her brow 'til I get back.' He didn't wait not one minute more.

"And wasn't an hour before he was at the door wit' a doctor—a white man, dressed nice. He looked at Ruby and felt on her and looked real serious there for a while. I thought, Oh, Lord, my chile, my chile. And he finally said, 'Thank goodness, ma'm, you've been spared.' He said it just like that and stopped. I didn't know what he meant. I said, 'Is she gon' be all right, doctor?' He said, 'Yes. I thought it might be cholera. But it's not. This baby doesn't have that deep sickness.' He tol' me to bathe her in water that wasn't too cool, and feed her nothin' for a day but lemon in water, and rub her little body wit' alcohol. Said the fever would break in a day. And it did. She started to sleep good, then eat good again. All the while Mr. Brown would run in and see how she was doin', how I was doin'. Brought me somethin' to eat—had Jennie's people fix it for me. He went out to my white folks' himself and spoke to cook and let her know what happened and said I would be comin' back to work soon as I could.

"I found out later it was Jennie seen to the whole thing. Seemed like Jennie didn't want me losin' my place 'cause she didn't want her Mister upset no kinda way. That doctor Mr. Brown brought was Jennie's doctor. He treated a lot o' women, colored and white, on the West Side there who were usin' they bodies some o' every kinda way. He got rid o' babies, or brought 'em into the world if it was too late, and saw to 'em bein' carried off someplace. Some o' these women mighta wanted to keep they baby, like I did, but they needed work, and they couldna got a place like the one I had. It wasn't easy, Hassalia, for nobody.

"After that Mr. Brown would stop to see how Ruby was doin', he said. And my landlady started showin' him up without sayin' nothin'. I found out later Mr. Brown and Jennie took care o' her, too—money, or scared her good, I don't know which.

"See, I didn't know it, Hassalia, but Mr. Brown set his eye on me. And the white man I work for, the day Ruby got sick and I didn't come to work, that very day he went to Jennie and tol' her I didn't come to work, and would she see to it. He didn't want no triflin' colored gal workin' for him and his wife. Tol' Jennie to find out whether I was doin' right or not. She the one sent Mr. Brown out to my house. Lord help me if I'da been there triflin'. Mr. Brown was a powerful strong man. And Jennie didn't take no triflin' lightly. May Ella didn't know what all she got me into, wit' her simple self. But there's always simple souls in this world, Hassalia, who start more mess than they ever see the end of.

"Jennie and Mr. Brown were waitin' for me to break. Turned out Jennie had three or four houses full o' young girls who worked for her doin' favors for men, some white, some colored. Let me slip on my job, or lose my baby, and Jennie and Mr. Brown would be right there to take me up into all they doin'. That's what they did: wait.

"See, Hassalia, a colored woman's body is always worth somethin' to somebody, 'til she gets too old, like I am now. Somebody wants it and will work it to the bone if they can. Work you to the bone, chile. Don't let nobody—not a Christian preacher or trash on the street—ever hold yo' body lightly, Hassalia. Don't allow it.

"But you forget. Ruby needed me then, but I didn't see it that way. I just nursed her and took care o' her, like I was s'posed to do, like my Mama done wit' me. But between the folks on my job gettin' me twelve hours a day and Mr. Brown after me the rest o' the time, I got caught up, and got cut off from Ruby—right then. I didn't see it for many a year, fallin' on my knees in church many and many a time not knowin' which way to turn. It was many and many a year, Hassalia, before I could see.

"Well, what happened was, Mr. Brown came to callin' and we started to carryin' on, and now and again he took me to some fancy place. Those were some fast dives and fast parties colored used to give we would go to, and I didn't mind 'cause I was wit' him. I wasn't thinkin' 'bout the man, really, 'cause I had sense enough to know he worked for Jennie and wasn't thinkin' 'bout marryin' nobody, and I didn't have that kind o' feelin' for him no way. I saw Jennie at the back o' all o' this, but I didn't think Jennie was rulin' *me*. She might be rulin' Mr. Brown, but what did that have to do wit' me? I was such a fool. Jennie was just waitin'.

"I came up one day carryin' a baby, yo' Uncle Jim. Lef' up to Jennie and Mr. Brown, he'da never seen the light o' day.

So, I told Mr. Brown, I said, 'I need to talk to that doctor again.' And he said, 'What for?' And I said, 'I missed. I'm sure to be carryin'.' I didn't want nothin' from this man right then, Hassalia, but I needed him right then, you understand? What was I gonna do? He said, 'Woman, I'll get the doctor, and you listen to what he say, hear?' And I said, 'What you mean? You know I'm gon' listen to what he say.' He said, 'Naw, I mean you *do* like he say.' And I said, still the fool that I was, 'You know I'm gon' do like the doctor tell me I'm s'posed to do when I'm carryin' a chile.' Then he said, 'You already got one chile. What you gon' do wit' another one?' I didn't say nothin'. He lef'. And the doctor came and looked at me and told me I was carryin' a chile for true, and he was gon' help me get rid of it.

"I put him out o' there. Right that minute. I said, 'You got to go now.' I stood up and he knew I meant what I was sayin'. At the door, he said, 'You can't wait much longer, remember that.' And then he lef'. No trouble. Just lef'. That's when I finally saw what him and Mr. Brown and Jennie were up to. That baby didn't mean nothin' to Mr. Brown. But he was hopin' all along I would turn out to be carryin' a baby, *his* baby. Hopin' I'd be so scared I'd do whatever him and Jennie said.

"He came to me the next day and said, 'Well, gal, you better go on and do what you s'posed to do. The doctor knows how to take care of the thing, and you'll be fine.' I said, 'Naw. I'm havin' this baby. You don't care nothin' for it, and you don't care nothin' for me, do you?' He got right mad. He said, 'Now, you listen to me, gal. Who looked after you and seen to you all this time? You know I work for Jennie, and you know she the one saw to you gettin' yo' job. And who helped you when yo' little gal there fell sick? Who brought you the doctor? Who went out to yo' white folks' place and tol' 'em not to treat you like another wild colored gal up from the country, and hold yo' place and not give it to nobody else? *We* did that. Me and Jennie. And now you gettin' ungrateful here, right sudden like.'

"I tol' him wasn't nothin' sudden. I was a woman looked after herself, didn't call on no man for nothin' 'lessen the man wanted to do it his own self. I looked him right in the eye, the rascal. But I was the one caught , Hassalia, not him. And he knew it. 'Fixin' to have you another baby, how you gon' keep yo' place? The folks ain't gon' wait for you to finish havin' no baby.' I knew he was right. Even if they wanted to wait on me, and liked me, and woulda held my place for me, Jennie would talk to Mr. Addleton and see to it I couldn't go back there. I knew right then I didn't have my place no mo'. And, like Mr. Brown said, a baby comin'.

"And it was his baby, Hassalia. He didn't want it, didn't want to claim it. So, right then—right that minute—it wasn't none o' his no mo'. It was mine. And I wasn't gonna let him have that baby, not even if he dropped down on his knees right there and begged me for it. Wasn't no way he could do me like he did—him and Jennie tryin' to trick me into livin' what they called the sportin' life—and care 'bout babies. They tricked anybody they could lay hold to.

"Jennie and him woulda turned me out into a West Side Chicago 'ho' if I'da let 'em. Lord don't want to think what woulda happened to yo' Mama—and yo' Uncle Jim wouldn't be here. Yo' Mama, they'da let her grow up 'round one o' these houses 'til she get up some size and then turn her out, too. I've seen it, Hassalia. Get a black gal young, you got her for life. Gal fourteen turnin' tricks before she knows what happened. By the time she's a woman—if she makes it without bein' cut in a razor fight, or beat up by some man who got drunk, or drunk herself to death—she ain't good for much else. No man wants her when he finds out what she's been doin'. If she had chil'ren, they gone, took away or livin' a wild life where they don't listen to they mama no way.

"That's the time a lot o' women turn to the Lord, lookin'

fo' they don't know what. That's who they trust. Nobody else. They put the cares o' this earth to one side, don't look on they troubles. Me, I come to the Lord when I was a little girl, like Mama taught me, but I strayed, Hassalia, I strayed. I'm not gon' lie to you, chile, not this evenin'.

"So, what was I gonna do? Mr. Brown lef' me for a fool, which Lord knows I was. Clarice was a good soul, and she came to see me and tol' me how Mr. Addleton tol' his Missus to let me go, I was a trifler, what was I doin' wit' that baby and no daddy for her, and all like that. Things can turn on you right sudden, Hassalia, when folks don't want you no more.

"I could sew, thank the Lord. Mama taught me that. My fingers could fly. Not like now, when my arthiritis has got me and I can't hardly lift a needle and thread without achin'. Back then, honey, I could go. And Clarice and May Ella started sendin' folks to me, and them folks sent more folks—all colored, at first, but later I got to workin' for white folks, too. Course I worked for white folks when I came here to Crawley. But back then I just sat in my little house and worked my fingers to the bone. Yo' Mama was good durin' the day. There were chil'ren 'round there to play wit'. I worked twelve hours a day, sewin'. I wouldn't work the whole day on Sunday. But I couldn't stop, Hassalia. The kinda piece work and dress makin' I was doin', I couldn't make no money unless I did a lot of it, fast. It got to the place I did things at home for a white folks' shirtwaist factory. They wouldna took me into they shop, but the lady would send me things to work on and I would get 'em done and she'd send somebody to pick 'em up. I bought myself a Singer sewin' machine. That was a happy day.

"I was scared, Hassalia, because here I had two chil'ren to do for, and myself, and my seamstressin' was just barely keepin' us goin'. It was a hard dollar and a hard day. Chil'ren get sick and I liked to go out o' my mind, 'cause I wasn't sure I had enough for medicine. Made they clothes, and could feed us. But that was 'bout all there was to it. Sometimes on Sunday I would go to church, and the church folks would help me out and try to send me a little bit o' work here and there. And I appreciated it, Lord knows I did. I thanked Him.

"But I was alone, honey. A man done spitefully used me. I didn't know how to act no more. Younguns pullin' on me was all I knew to think about.

"After your Uncle Jim reached up to some little size—he was four—we moved here to Crawley. Little country town. What here lately they callin' 'the suburbs', wit' white folks buildin' a lot o' new ranch houses. But for us, the colored, Crawley was just a country town, like country towns we seen and done come from. And white folks run the town. Wasn't nothin' new about that.

"Just a handful of us when I first came here. You see the church over there, but back then the church was just colored folks' houses, where we'd meet. On a good Sunday there'd be fifty of us, countin' the chil'ren. We'd set up in folks' livin' rooms or basements. Clear out the space, rent us some chairs, preacher could carry the pulpit and the altar wit' him in his car. Reverend Wilkes it was at the time. We finally got to usin' the Cryers' basement. They didn't have no chil'ren, so it wasn't too much trouble for them to keep church, the way we called it. We kep' on raisin' money 'til we bought the chairs we needed, and the fans and the hymn books. Finally we got enough together to get the folks at the bank to loan us some money, and that's how we got our little buildin' over here.

"So, here I was. I had the good feelin' o' the church and the church folks. They wasn't no way I could make enough money seamstressin' all by itself. I kep' it up, but I couldn't get enough work, even from white folks. So, I took in laundry and started doin' day work. By that time yo' Mama and yo' Uncle Jim were in school, so I could work in the daytime when I needed to. I would work three, four days a week out, the rest o' the time in, doin' laundry or sewin'. Mr. and Mrs. Tillman rented out they basement, and that's where me and the chil'ren lived. I didn't know right off what the church folks would say. May Ella was the one who tol' Mrs. Tillman 'bout me—her and May Ella's mama come from the same town—and seemed like she didn't mind. Her and her husband were right decent to me and the chil'ren. Didn't mind the noise the chil'ren kep' up. Let 'em play in the yard. And let me string up more clotheslines for my laundry I took in.

"When folks would ask me 'bout the chil'ren's daddy, I'd say, 'Well, both they daddies felt like they didn't wanna be wit' us no more. And that's fine.' I looked 'em in the eye when I said it, but I never knew if I could hold my eye steady the whole time. Christian folks can be hard on you, Hassalia. To this day a whole lot o' the folks I knew back then when the church wasn't even a buildin' yet still ain't easy speakin' to me *except* at church. And I ain't never been in they house, neither. I'm tellin' you, chile, a Christian's funny. You can't get but so close. It took me a long time before I knew that. By the time I did, it was too late to do me any good. Everything comes too late, Hassalia. By the time you see, it's too late to do anything about what's worryin' you."

Ma Rhetta looked tired, but her voice wasn't tired. It was like she had to finish telling me something if I would just listen. It was the last time—besides her telling me to wear a skirt—she asked me for anything right up until she died three years later.

I was 15 this hot summer night, and it was only a year since I started having my period. I started late. I found out how babies got here from my friends, mostly. Me and Mama talked about it, too, but I couldn't ask Mama too many questions. It would be like I was worrying her, 'cause when it came to men and babies Mama had enough worries with Daddy, I knew. So, I didn't make Mama talk about it. Now I think maybe she woulda if I'da just asked her like I really needed to know, which I did. But back then I couldn't stand hearing her tear my Daddy down, and she knew that. All I'da got was slapped if I gave her any mouth about him, which I would have.

What I didn't see that night was, Ma Rhetta was talking to me like I knew what a man was and what was s'posed to happen between a man and a woman, even if it hardly ever did. She treated me like a woman. That was the night I started, even if it was only started, really turning into one. I wasn't about to give up wearing pants right then—they were comfortable. But I started to learn that night what Mama couldn't teach me, not then: what a woman goes through to be treated with some kinda respect. Ma Rhetta wasn't just my grandmother anymore after that night. I got to see how she was a woman *before* she was my grandmother.

She scared me that night, but when she asked me if I was tired and wanted her to stop, I just said, "No, ma'm. Go on, please." I don't know why I said "please" like that, like I was asking for another piece of fudge.

I keep wondering now—I didn't think about it then, except way, way in the back of my mind, where I couldn't hear myself think—if Aunt Fanny did come into the living room and sit in the chair next to the open screen door and listen. If she did, I wonder what she thought when she heard Ma Rhetta talk about her daddy. Sometimes I hope Fanny was there. Other times I hope she wasn't. Mostly, now, I hope she was.

Ma Rhetta. "Now, yo' Aunt Fanny's comin', that was a bunch o' foolishness. I don't say it 'cause I was triflin', me nor Fanny's daddy neither. Still and all, didn't nobody hold no gun to our heads. That's why I say it was a lot o' foolishness. We knew better. But we went ahead anyway. Your Aunt Fanny's strugglin' for respect like she is is her fightin' 'gainst me and what I did all them years ago. White and colored both are havin' trouble respectin' Fanny. It grieves me. But I didn't make the world. I think Fanny thinks I did. Or coulda made it over for her into a place where she'd be like everybody else. That's what Fanny acts like she wants. She don't. Nobody does. But when things ain't right for you, you can always say, "My mama and daddy shoulda done so-and-so or shouldna done such-and-such. Then I'd be like everybody else." But them folks you tryin' to be like, they mama and daddy didn't know what to do, either. And all the while you tryin' to be like everybody else, the truth is, somebody's thinkin' they might be better off if they was you. You could tell 'em different, but would they listen? It don't do me no good to talk this way, 'cause Fanny ain't ever gon' see it no way but I done her wrong.

"Anyway, he wasn't what I was lookin' for, I will say that. He wasn't what I was no ways expectin'. I didn't know nothin' 'bout no man like him. Sylvester T. Niles, that's who it was."

My eyes jumped, and Ma Rhetta saw 'em. She knew why. I knew Mr. Niles' son, the man I called Mr. Niles (first name of Coleman), and his wife, Geneva, and their daughter, Aletha. Letha—that's what we called her—went to school with me. We didn't hardly have anything to say to each other. I thought she was stuck up. She acted like she thought I was common. Her granddaddy and Ma Rhetta— I never woulda thought that.

Ma Rhetta. "I know you can't hardly believe that. I couldn't hardly either, when it was happenin'. But I brought it down on myself. To start off, he was married. Cora. Funny thing was, I never had no truck wit' her, but whenever I did see her I liked her all right. I didn't have nothin' to say 'gainst the woman.

"She was sickly, po' thing. She was just weak. Couldn't stand the hot, couldn't stand the cold. Scared all the time. Nervous. Arthiritis got her early and wouldn't let her go, she used to say. And then she had bad headaches and back-aches. Pretty thing, too. Had her fine way, like a lady. Sylvester used to say she wasn't cold, she just didn't ever warm up no more. The life was out of her. Cared about the boy, Coleman, when she could. But most o' the time she couldn't do much o' anything.

"So, for a long time Sylvester just waited, and his feelin' for her kep' him all right. He didn't think about nothin' else, nobody else, he tol' me.

"But one day he came from work—he worked in the city, in a music store; even learned on the sly how to tune pianos—and there was Cora, sittin' in a chair waitin' for him, and she didn't have nothin' on, not a stitch. She just looked at him when he came through the screen door and said, 'Sylvester, I'm not your wife anymore, am I? You don't want to see me like this any more, do you?'

"Sylvester tol' me it was the saddest thing he ever saw, 'cause it *didn't* matter to him any more, but he never said it to himself 'til she said it, just like that, sittin' in the chair wit' no clothes on, knowin' he didn't want her. He went and got her a bathrobe and helped her cover up. She cried and cried. Not loud. Lowlike, and moanin'.

"So, when him and me started up, I didn't want to do it, Hassalia. I'd been knowin' the two of 'em since I came to Crawley, and didn't pay him no particular mind. Sylvester was a gentleman, fine-lookin' man. But no woman woulda just gone up and started talkin' to him. He wouldna stood for that. When I first met him, him and her were still comin' out to church together. She'd be wit' him, wearin' white gloves, and tiny little shoes. Brown-skinned woman, pretty, hair done up beautiful—it was gray mixed in it, but it was good-lookin', and she fixed it so nice. Sylvester would be in a good, dark suit. You just wouldn't think o' sayin' nothin' out o' the way to neither one of 'em. And they son, Coleman, all smart and handsome. He played piano for the church choir sometimes, and recitals, too.

"Well, I never did think twice 'bout sayin' nothin' out of the way to Sylvester, even after Cora got down sick and stopped comin' to church. He would still come.

"You still thought about her wit' him even when you didn't see her no more. You could almost see her in her white gloves and her arm in his, even when he would walk into church by himself. He was a deacon and all, so the folks in the church gave him all kind o' respect. He knew a lot about music, too, so they listened to him that way. He tuned the pianos at the church.

"Truth was, he was a janitor in that music place in the city. He didn't lie 'bout it. Everybody knew. The white folks there taught him a little bit 'bout tunin' pianos. He had the ear for it, he used to tell me. And he liked to play a little himself. He was glad to see to it Coleman got music lessons.

"But Sylvester didn't fool himself. He knew there wasn't no way a Negro was gonna be goin' 'round tunin' white folks' pianos in they concert halls or in they houses. The folks wouldna trusted a colored man, or even let him in the front door. He loved music, but he knew he didn't have the gift for it like Coleman did, so he didn't even try.

"The day him and me got started was real peculiar. We moved out o' Mrs. Tillman's basement and were livin' up over Mrs. Rodgers' house—kinda like up in the attic, but it was big, ran the length o' the whole house. We had four nice rooms up there, me and the chil'ren, and there was lots o' heat in the wintertime. Summertime it was way too hot, but we just opened the windows and tried every way we could think of to keep cool.

"Well, one day I was sittin' there fannin' myself in the heat—it was summertime and both the chil'ren were off somewhere playin' and I sat down to cool myself off after doin' my ironin'—when I heard this scratchin' at my screen door. I didn't hear nobody come up the steps. So, when I heard the scratchin' I thought it must be Mrs. Rodgers come up to ask me for somethin'. She didn't visit, so I knew it would always be to borrow somethin' or to come for the rent money. So, I'm thinkin' it musta been her. I could see through the screen door but I didn't even look that way. I was just talkin' to the ceilin', holdin' somethin' cool in one hand and fannin' myself wit' the other, when I heard this scratchin' at the door and I says, 'Come on in, Sister Rodgers.' Didn't think nothin' 'bout what I was sayin'.

"The door opened, and there was Sylvester, breathin' so fast I thought he was gonna fall out. I said, 'Brother Niles, is that you?' He couldn't say nothin' for a minute. Just stood there breathin', sweat pourin' down his face. And he said, 'Sister, can you please come and help me, quick? My wife is ailin' and I don't know what to do for her. I ran down the street lookin' for somebody, and I heard your radio and came on up here. Didn't look like nobody else was home all along the street. Or they must be asleep. Would you come look at her for me, please?' They just lived up the street, four houses from Mrs. Rodgers'—you know, Hassalia, where Coleman lives now. Sylvester came down the street lookin' for somebody and I was the first one he found. They had a phone, but when I got there I saw why he didn't want to use that to call the doctor, not yet.

"Cora was startin' to hurt herself, po' thing. Got holt to Sylvester's straight razor and cut herself all up and down her legs. They were little tiny cuts, all inside her thighs right up next to her private parts. And she said to him, 'You don't want me no more, so this what I'm gon' do to myself. I don't want you to even look up here between my legs no more. I'm gon' make it so ugly up here you won't want to look. You don't have to look. It's all right.'

"When me and Sylvester got there she was sittin' in the front room in a chair with her dressing gown open, wit' nothin' else on, and there was blood all over her and on her hands, and all over the chair.

"She said to him, 'Who is this woman you brought into my house? She the one you want instead o' me? I told him'—she looked right at me when she said this part, wasn't even shamefaced—'if he don't want me he don't have to have me. Ain't nobody gon' have me no more. He don't even have to look no more if he don't want to. He don't have to look.' And she closed her gown back up and started to cry.

"I pulled up a little hassock next to her and sat there and held her hand and talked to her for a little bit. I said, 'Now, honey'—I didn't call her by name, 'cause I didn't want to upset her, like I was tryin' to get in her bid'ness. She didn't know me all that well, and I was tryin' to act like I was some o' any old body he mighta found out in the street to help him. It was funny, but right then, even though she was hurtin' bad as she was, I felt like I didn't belong in that house, almost like me and Sylvester were carryin' on—and we weren't, not then.

"So, I said, 'Now, honey, let me just see how you doin' here. It looks like to me you hurt yo'self. We gonna ask this man'—me and her are friends now, right quick, and Sylvester is a stranger got no bid'ness—'to step outta here.' I said to Sylvester, 'Would you step out of the room, please, while me and her talk?' I was talkin' to him like I was a nurse or somebody and knew what I was s'posed to do, which I didn't. But I wanted to calm her, and I knew I couldn't wit' him standin' there. He went into the kitchen.

"Then I said, 'Now, let me see what you did here, honey.' I was gentle. I knew it wasn't gonna do no good to get mad wit' her or get her scared. I knew we had to get her quiet so we could stop the bleedin' and put some alcohol on them cuts and get the doctor.

"She showed me what she did. She kept cryin' and sayin' how Sylvester didn't want her no more. I kept sayin' a pretty woman like her had no bid'ness talkin' like that, how her husband musta wanted her, how Coleman needed her, and once we got her all cleaned up and got the doctor over there she could rest and would be fine.

"She cried to me, and then she was quiet. She said, 'Oh, look what I did to myself.' And I said, 'Don't you worry none, now, honey. I'm gon' see to it the doctor comes. Let me go out in the kitchen and get some cloths and some cool water and we'll start washin' up.'

"I went out into the kitchen, and Sylvester was standin' there, already lookin' so grateful. He said, 'I was hopin' you would get her quiet. I couldn't do nothin' with her. She wouldn't let me come near her.' I said, 'Well, I got her still now. But I got to clean her up before she gets a bad infection. The alcohol or the iodine is gonna sting bad. It's gonna take me a little while. Go get the doctor'. We were whisperin'. He understood. He slipped out the back.

"I found some clean tea towels and got a bowl and ran some water in it, first hot then plenty o' cool, and took it back in the front room. She was sittin' there holdin' her head. I said, 'Now, honey, let's see what we can do.' 'All right,' she said, real low. She wouldn't lift up her head, like she didn't want to look at me. I made her sit up and open up her gown, and I got a good look at what she done. There were cuts all over her legs. She got so close to her private parts she scared me. I thought at first blood was comin' from there. It wasn't, but there woulda been if me and Sylvester got there one minute later.

"I said, 'Now, honey, let me just wash you off a little bit, and then we'll put some alcohol on you and you'll feel better. All right?' 'Yes.' She said it like a chile.

"The po' thing was as strong as she could be while I

cleaned her up. Funny thing was, she smelled good, like sweet soap. It was like she just bathed. Maybe she was takin' a bath when she decided to do it, I don't know. After I got the blood cleaned off, I looked in the bathroom and found some alcohol and some cotton. I said, 'Now, honey, they ain't no way this ain't gonna hurt, but we got to do this, or you gon' get infected. Let me try a little bit o' alcohol, then a little bit o' this mercurochrome.'

"It was the hardest time I ever had nursin' anybody. Even when chil'ren are sick and don't want you to fuss wit' 'em, they know they oughta do like you sayin' if they want to get better.

"But this alcohol *hurt* this woman. I knew it hurt. I went slow as I could. And she would tremble and suck in her breath and moan every time I touched a piece o' cotton wit' the alcohol on it to one o' them cuts. But she sat there. And she didn't curse me or tell me to stop. She knew I had to do it. It took me a half hour. I would wait between each cut a little bit to let her get back to herself. Then I'd say, 'Please, honey, I know it's hurtin', but let me do the next one.' I didn't know how soon Sylvester was gon' get back wit' no doctor, and I knew those cuts shouldn't wait all open like they were.

"And, 'cause I treated his wife decent one day when she was in trouble—that was how Sylvester and me started up. It was real foolishness. We were in a small town, wit' a handful o' colored folks. Everybody knew everybody. In the church you could find out everybody's bid'ness—find out a lot 'bout folks who never set foot in church. There wasn't no way to slip and do much without folks knowin'. Me and Sylvester both knew that. We talked 'bout it. But you just talkin' 'cause you scared. He started comin' by the house late evenin's when the chil'ren were asleep. Yo' Mama was nine and yo' Uncle Jim was seven. I explained it to the both o' them later. Ruby first. But that didn't happen 'til yo' Aunt

Fanny was almost born. Yo' Uncle Jim didn't know all that was goin' on right then. He put it together later, wit' yo' Mama helpin'.

"Sylvester was married, wit' a sickly wife. Some folks used to say she wasn't right in the head, but that wasn't so. She couldn't do for herself no more. Sylvester finally had to have his sister to move in wit' 'em and help. She came up from North Carolina.

"Sylvester knew folks wouldn't take to him slippin' 'round wit' a woman who washed clothes for a livin', had two chil'ren and no daddy to show for 'em. It didn't look right no kinda way. And we weren't careful like we shoulda been. I came up carryin' yo' Aunt Fanny. Fantelle. He picked that name for her.

"By that time, a lot o' folks knew, but didn't nobody say nothin' to him or to me. Folks just made up they minds. Didn't nobody dare say nothin', 'cause they knew we weren't gonna stop. Then when I came up carryin' yo' Aunt Fanny there wasn't too much they could say.

"Sylvester was good to me. But we were foolish. We didn't think 'bout how we were gonna keep on. I made him happy. But he couldn't do nothin' 'bout his wife. They had little Coleman. He was only five then, but some day somebody would tell him. Folks said what a shame it was. But they sorta went through the whole thing wit' Sylvester and her, not me. Sylvester was a deacon at the church, and we thought the board o' deacons would make him step out. They knew I was carryin' his chile. But they never did ask him off the board. I look back now and I can see that they never woulda. Sylvester was one o' the people started the church. I was bad, not him.

"What was the man gonna do, Hassalia? He surely wasn't gon' leave a sick wife and his little boy for me, wit' two chil'ren o' my own and he didn't know who they daddy was—and I tol' him he wasn't never gonna find out, so don't ask me. He couldna lef' his wife for a woman who would say that to him.

"He was shy. I asked him when he stopped havin' any feelin' for his wife, and he said he couldn't rightly say when. She just couldn't stand to have him next to her. Told him she was dirty and ailin' and couldn't no man want her.

"He didn't stop seein' me for the longest time after Fanny was born. We carried on for a while, but after we stopped that part of it he would still come by and bring things to Fanny and to the other chil'ren.

"Ruby and Jim knew what was goin' on. But Sylvester wasn't comin' 'round any more when Fanny got up some size and started askin' me who was her daddy.

"I lied. I couldn't do nothin' else, Hassalia. Ruby and Jim went 'long wit' me. They knew I had to lie to Fanny. She couldna stood knowin' her daddy lived four doors down the street and was married to somebody else wit' a boy o' they own. Fanny wouldna known what to do about that. I started goin' back to church, and seein' to it the chil'ren got to Sunday school some o' the time. I wasn't as good 'bout church as I was s'posed to be, because I knew how bad folks talked about me. And they haven't stopped right up 'til now. It was hard to go to church and sit there. So, for a long while I didn't go. I just wouldn't let them folks be the boss o' me, Hassalia. I was workin' every day for white folks who were the boss o' me. Me and my chil'ren wouldn't eat 'lessen I took in they laundry and cleaned they houses and looked after they chil'ren. I wasn't gon' let colored folks be the boss o ' me, too. They can set the whole church against you, Hassalia, and make you feel like the evillest kinda woman who ever was. That's what they did to me. Not to Sylvester. To me. And I didn't want Fanny to go through that all over again, not even in her mind.

"But she did anyway. She musta figured it out. Been figurin' it out. I tol' her her daddy was a salesman come through town like that drummer I used to know. I tol' her he was a good man but we weren't gonna hear from him no more. Like none o' these daddies. And Ruby and Jim didn't say nothin'. For a while I used to be 'fraid they mighta tol' her just to be evil, like chil'ren can be. But they tol' me they didn't, and I believed 'em. They knew well as I did Fanny couldna stood that then.

"Well, when she was sixteen, it came out. There was no way it coulda stayed in, I guess. Your Uncle Grease was born by that time. Yo' Mama had Esther and Johnnie by then. And Izell was already sorta here and sorta not, there wasn't no certain way o' tellin'.

"So, some o' the colored girls at school got to talkin' 'bout babies in our house and where they came from. One of 'em tol' Fanny they didn't believe what she tol' 'em 'bout her daddy bein' long gone. This girl's mama tol' her Fanny's daddy was right here in Crawley. She said to me, 'You mean my daddy's right here and won't claim me?'

"Right then I tol' her 'bout Sylvester. To this day, I don't know if I should or shouldna. She listened to everything, then she said, 'Why did you lie to me?' I said, 'Fanny, you woulda wanted to know yo' daddy, you know you woulda. You woulda gone down to his house and been tryin' to talk to him. And he had a wife and a son, and he couldna done nothin' 'bout it. He'da wanted to, Fanny, but he couldna done nothin'. He wasn't a rich man, Fanny. He had all he could do to keep up his family. He did little things for you when he could. And he tried to help me out as much as he could. But he didn't have nothin' for you, Fanny, he didn't *have* it.' She cried and cried about it.

"She been mad at me ever since. Tried in her own little way to get back at me ever since. Thinks everybody in this town is lookin' at her and laughin' at her 'cause o' me. And 'cause I lied to her. Thinks I made her look like a fool. But that's not what I did, Hassalia. I was the fool, not her. Me and Sylvester. I used to ask myself sometime what it woulda been like if I'da met Sylvester before he was married, and if we'da got married. I wasn't the kinda woman Sylvester woulda married, Hassalia. He liked Cora. Refined. She had airs, was a lady. Pretty hands. I was a maid, a washwoman. I could sew and cook and clean. She carried herself all dainty and tol' him how nice his music was and all.

"Least when they started out, she made him feel like somebody. I made him feel good. By the time he met me I don't think he knew one from the other—maybe I was makin' him feel like a different somebody. But I was just doin' what she couldn't do no more, makin' him feel good. That's what I was there for, time I came along. But it woulda been the same thing if he'da met me before. He'da been lookin' for a woman like her. And he'da found her and lef' me for her.

"The most peculiar thing about it is, Fanny's like her. Cora, I mean. Sylvester's wife. Always has been. And she's like Sylvester, too. But I see Cora in her. Is it there, or is it just me thinkin' it's there?

"I know I been hard on Fanny sometimes, Hassalia. But Fanny needed lookin' after after she found out 'bout her daddy. All her life since then, she needed lookin' after. Does she know it? Is she the littlest bit grateful? That's why I gave her so much hell when she run off wit' and come back from that white soldier. She never woulda done such if she'da knowed how to look after herself, not let no man take advantage o' her. Spite, it was. Tryin' to disgrace me, she was.

"Well, she found out for good and for fair what a man will do, colored or white, don't make no nevermind. Fanny's not a girl, but she wants to go on actin' like one. That's what I'm tryin' to tell you, Hassalia. You ain't no girl no more. You're next door to a woman. Ain't no man gon' give you nothin'—not kindness nor a crust o' bread—just 'cause o' what you got between yo' legs, no matter how much he tells you he loves it. If he gives, he's gon' take, chile, from deeper down than you even know is there. Once a man's been between yo' legs and you really want this man, somethin' else opens up, Hassalia, somethin' you didn't know was there. *That's* where he takes from. It's a man's nature. Take and run, most of 'em. Marry you and still stray, one way or another—it can be whiskey or cars or gamblin' or goin' to church—it don't have to be another woman. You can get you a daddy, Hassalia, but that don't mean you gon' keep him. A steady man is a hard thing to hold. You find one, I say, Hold tight, honey, and don't let go.

PART THREE

RUBY, 1957

She said, You are the granddaughter
of an African, and you have
inherited a way of being.
And her eyes stayed on mine, Anninho,
until all her words and memory
and fears and the tenderness
ran through me like blood...
That was the moment when I became
my grandmother and she became me
Do you know what I mean?
Yes.
Our spirits were one.
Yes.
But it was more than that.
Yes. We are never alone.
We keep everything.
Yes....

—Gayl Jones
Song for Anninho

MA RHETTA. "THAT'S ENOUGH, NOW, HONEY. That's enough." It seemed like Ma Rhetta was talking to herself. She wasn't looking at me. She started swinging, gentle. I could tell she wasn't gonna talk anymore, not right then. I was waiting to hear about Uncle Grease, who his daddy was. But she wasn't gonna tell me, not then. I found out about Gregory's daddy later. But by then there was a whole lot I'd been seeing that I wouldna believed if you'da told me on a stack of Bibles. Everything happens too late, the way Ma Rhetta said. I know now what she meant. I didn't then, not that night on the porch, not right up 'til the day, four years after that, when we lost people like flies.

I wish I coulda seen what was coming. Wouldna been anything I coulda done, prob'ly. Maybe. I don't know. I was still just a chile, and nobody wants to listen to their chile. Don't need a chile telling 'em nothing. By now I got sense enough to listen to mine, but then that's too late, too, so Ma Rhetta's still right. She was right all along.

I guess she couldna done nothing to help Mama, either. Mama wasn't of much mind to be listening to Ma Rhetta, it seemed to me then. She always taught us to respect Ma Rhetta, but I never could see where she let Ma Rhetta tell her much. I couldn't *see*. But that didn't mean Ma Rhetta *wasn't* telling Mama what to do in her own way, and it didn't mean Mama wasn't struggling with Ma Rhetta all the time I was growing up, right in the same house with 'em.

One night, just before Ma Rhetta got bad sick—it was about 3 o'clock in the morning—I was in bed and I woke up. To this day I don't know why. I don't remember hearing anything. I just woke up. I could feel something going on in the house. Ma Rhetta was still getting outta bed every day and all, but she wasn't at herself.

More and more, we could all see, she took to just sitting and staring out the big kitchen window on all of Jim's junk in the back yard. Time was she'd go out in the yard every once in a while and look around to see what Jim had brought in lately. The back yard was always changing, with old stuff going out and new old stuff coming in. It was all old, but we would call it new when it first came in. Jim would say, "Got a nice new dining table coming in today. Gon' go on out to the highway and pick it up." It mighta been 50 years old, something some white folks decided they didn't want anymore, no notion to keep, and Jim woulda found out about it, or they woulda called him up and told him.

Anyway, Jim was just calling it new. He knew he needed to look it over real good before he could think about what he was gon' do with it—whether to sell it to colored or white. "Junk is funny," Jim used to say. "What one somebody can't stand, somebody else is tickled to get. It's old, but it's new to them. You can't say what wears out first, the folks or the thing."

So, Jim was always talking about something "new" coming in, and when you'd look at it it might be so old and dirty and beat up and full of knicks and cuts and scars and scrapes and holes and stains you wouldn't touch it. But Jim could fix it up, or have somebody else fix it up, or leave it just like it was, and sell it.

He'd sit and figure how much he wanted to do to it, whether white folks or one of the good colored families would want it if he did it, whether some poor white folks or some of the rest of the colored would take it if he left it alone, and how much any of 'em would pay.

Jim got from all over. He would make runs for 50 miles around. There were back alleys in certain towns Jim knew about, he would drive to that town just to go look in that alley, 'cause some folks he knew there would leave stuff out for him to look at, and if he wanted it he could take it and pay the folks later. This was how the yard used to fill up and up and up. It would never be empty, so a lot of folks would think nothing was going on. They'd see Jim sitting around, sometimes for days, and it looked like he wasn't doing anything. But he was figuring. Sometimes he'd tell you, sometimes he wouldn't. He'd say, "I ain't got time right now." And me or Mama or Ma Rhetta or anybody with good sense would know to let him be. Even if he was just sitting in the kitchen drinking coffee and smoking a cigarette, you better let him alone. He was thinking what to do about *something* out in that yard.

Sometimes Ma Rhetta would sit and look out at it, too. Jim didn't have to look at something but one time and he remembered it. He could tell you about anything out in that yard without even looking up from his coffee. But Ma Rhetta would sit there looking out at it all and study it.

And time by time she'd say something like, "Jim, what you gon' do with that nice looking Hotpoint you got out there?"—some washing machine she'd lay her eye on. Jim would say, "Don't know." He might not say any more. And Ma Rhetta wouldn't ask him any more, not right then. She'd wait. Give him a few minutes, drinking his coffee and chewing him a sweet roll and smoking his Lucky Strikes. Then he'd say, "Some folks over in Elmwood looking for them one, I know, but them niggers don't want to pay nothing for nothing, and that's a good little ol' Hotpoint out there. I don't know no white folks looking for one right now, and I don't want to leave it too long. Parts on that thing'll rust up on you, you leave it go. So, maybe I'll carry it on over to them colored folks. Shoot, these niggers is subject to have a party behind something that pretty and white coming into they house. These folks have to struggle to keep 'em some heat in the wintertime, they little house is so raggedy, next door to falling down. And they ain't gon' have no money. Never do. I may just as well say I'm giving it to 'em, 'cause they ain't got no money and can't keep the little bit they do get. House full of kids. That skinny little lady would jump up and down she get her a Hotpoint like that, never mind no dryer to go with it. She ain't gon' worry about no dryer. These niggers so ignorant I'm not sure they know an automatic clothes washer *got* a dryer go with it. This lady just be happy to get rid of that nasty wringer washer she got up in there. One of her kids got his arm mashed up in the wringers one day. Had to carry him to the hospital. Chile's arm swole up, doctors didn't know what they was gon' do. Turned out didn't break no bones. But she got two littler than that one, and one of them subject to stick they arm in that ol' wringer one of these mornings she doing her washing. So, maybe I will carry that Hotpoint on over to them folks."

He would chew on his sweet roll a minute and sip him some coffee. "I hate to do it, 'cause I don't want to let it go for near about nothing, which is all they gon' be able to pay. I'm gon' stretch that nigger 'til he holler, that's what I'm gon' do. He gon' tell me he ain't got but fifteen dollars a mont' lef' over from his check, and his babies need 'em some shoes, and some kinda mess like that he gon' be telling me. I could make him pay me fifty, even if it takes three, four months for him to do it. But I'd be running over there every mont' to get the rest of my money, and wouldn't get nothing but a lie. I'll get thirty out of that fool. Umh! Hate to let a nice little Hotpoint go for that. But that's what I just might do."

And he would finish his coffee and his cigarette and his sweet roll. Ma Rhetta might ask him about something else out in the yard or she might not. They'd just go on sitting there, the both of 'em, wondering about all that junk. Where it came from and where it was going.

So, this particular night, I just woke up. I laid there for a while. Still didn't hear nothing. I got up and went downstairs, halfway telling myself I was gon' get myself something out of the Kelvinator. I went down to the kitchen and there was Ma Rhetta, wide awake, sitting in the big kitchen window, staring out into the yard. It was almost pitch black out there. You could see in the yard a little bit, 'cause of the street light, but there wasn't any moon. A water heater on the back porch had a little light in it, and that's how I saw her sitting there at first. I saw her soon as I came through the kitchen door. She was so still, I didn't turn on the light. I could hear her breathing. She wasn't feeling at herself there lately, and I thought maybe she got up to get herself a cool glass of water out of the icebox. But it didn't seem like she was in pain, sitting up straight in the chair. I let her be. My eyes were getting used to the dark, so I could see her halo of hair around her head.

Then she made this sound. It was something like a moan and something like she was crying. It didn't come out of her throat, it came from down in her chest. A deep sigh, it was. She only did it once. She shifted around in the chair a little bit, and then went back to looking out the window.

I still didn't say anything. I went back out into the dining room and made some noise so she would hear me coming. I didn't want her to think I was standing there watching and heard her sigh or cry or whatever that sound was. When I got to the kitchen door I didn't turn on the light, and she didn't turn around. But the way she hunched up her shoulders I knew she heard me.

"Ruby?" she said.

"No, it's me, Ma Rhetta." She still didn't turn around in the chair. Was she crying?

"Oh, Hassalia, that you?"

"Yes, Ma'm."

"What you doin' up, girl?"

"Came down to get some of that Kool-Aid in the Kelvinator left over from supper." She didn't say anything. "Can I turn on the light?"

"Go ahead, girl."

I turned on the light and got a glass, went to the Kelvinator and poured some Kool-Aid. But before I went over and sat next to her, I went back and turned out the light again. If she was crying I didn't think she would want me to see her. I wanted to see if she was all right. But I didn't want to embarrass her if she wasn't feeling good and didn't want me to know about it.

"You want some?"

"No, daughter." Sometimes she would call me "daughter", even though I was her granddaughter. She would do the same thing with Esther, and was starting to do it with Beetsy, too, and Beetsy was her great granddaughter.

I sat down next to her with my glass of Kool-Aid. Finally I said, "Ma Rhetta, you all right?"

"Yes, daughter. I'm all right."

"What you doing up so late?"

"I don't rightly know. I been sittin' here better part of the evenin'. Went to bed 9 o'clock and couldn't sleep no kind o' way. Got up about 11:00 and come out here. Been sittin' here ever since."

"What you thinking about, Ma Rhetta?" I don't know what kinda fool I was to be asking that. And I don't think I was a big enough fool to think she was gonna tell me, just like that.

"Nothin', daughter. Too much. I just can't put away the cares of the day."

First off, I thought maybe she was talking about what Dr. Clay told her. He was there that day. So I said, "Dr. Clay said you was gonna be all right, Ma Rhetta, if we just see to you resting like you should and eating proper."

"Yes, daughter, I know." I could tell by the way she said that she wasn't thinking about Dr. Clay. Or maybe she was thinking about Dr. Clay and the medicine and all, and staying well so she wouldn't go to the hospital—but that wasn't what was on her mind. Ma Rhetta was looking something in the face, staring at all that junk out in the yard you could barely see in the dark. I even wondered if maybe the little bit of light from the water heater over in the corner mighta been enough to throw Ma Rhetta's reflection up on the window, so maybe she was sitting there looking at her own face. But in all of that darkness? After I thought for a minute I doubted it.

I sat there sipping Kool-Aid. I wanted one of those oatmeal cookies Mama baked that were in the cookie jar—and I didn't. While I was thinking about it I asked Ma Rhetta, "Why do you think Daddy doesn't come back home, Ma Rhetta?"

She waited a minute and gave me a look. A sad look. Sad for me. But I didn't feel sad for me. I felt sad for her. Then she said, "Men don't light, Hassalia. Don't stay nowhere. Here one day and gone the next."

But what about *me*, I wanted to say. Doesn't my daddy want to see *me*? Instead, I said, "I'm gonna stay off those railroads, Ma Rhetta. Go somewhere on the train you don't know what's gonna happen. You're subject never to come back. Or if you do, look what can happen to you, even if you only go away on a train for a little while, like Aunt Fanny and that soldier."

"Men don't light, Hassalia. Colored or white, don't make no difference. They all find someplace to run to."

"What good is a man, anyway, Ma Rhetta?"

First she cut her eyes at me. Then she just laughed and laughed, chuckling low so long I knew that was the only answer I was gonna get, bold as I thought I was to be asking a womanish question like that.

A few weeks after that night Ma Rhetta had her stroke and took to her bed. She never got up from it. I've been without her ever since that time. I've never missed anybody so bad.

*

After Ma Rhetta died, Mama got like I didn't know her. It wasn't just that she got quiet. Mama was real quiet—dangerous quiet—from when I was a chile. She could step up behind you and you wouldn't know it. When I wanted to be by myself in the house I would go to my room or down in the basement or way up in the attic and close the door. I had to, because I knew if I was in a room by myself with the door open, Mama could slip up on me. She was just *there* when I looked around.

Mama wasn't small. She had wide hips and big breasts, and she was built strong in the legs, the thighs, the arms. She wasn't fat, but there was a lot to her. She was dark, like me, and could wave her hair pretty when she wanted to. A little while before, she got glasses for when she had to read, and that used to hurt her feelings, her pride, first off. She'd lose 'em all the time, leave 'em all over the house, break 'em, not clean 'em, not use 'em. But let her want to read how to do something off a box or look at her newspaper come evening or play at reading the Bible (Ma Rhetta was the steady Bible reader in that house, not Mama), she'd need 'em and hate 'em. But there they'd be, sitting on her nose, making her look proper, like Mama never looked.

Mama got more quiet after Ma Rhetta died. I didn't ask her about it 'cause you couldn't. Not me. Not anybody I ever saw. If I got to asking Mama how she was feeling, before too long she was gonna get around to my daddy, and don't get Mama started on that.

When I was little she would talk about Daddy, 'cause we used to see him every once in a while. He would come in all dressed up in a suit and lift me up and carry me on his back, and bring me dolls and things that I didn't know what to do with. Some of 'em were big toy animals, like horses and giraffes. And he'd buy me candy and take me to the show to see color cartoons all afternoon. He'd have somebody with him, a gentleman friend he worked with, not a woman—Mama wouldna stood for that—and the gentleman would have a car and they'd take me for rides. We'd stop by the side of the road and buy watermelons and bring 'em back to the house and they'd get cool in the icebox and we'd eat 'em after supper. I could eat all I wanted. After he'd go Mama would tell me he was coming back, and how handsome he was and how he wanted to be with us but had to work on the road. She'd keep up like that for a little while. Then a whole lot of weeks would go by and she wouldn't hear anything from Daddy, and she'd know she wasn't gonna 'til he decided to show up again. I just knew he was coming back 'cause he was coming back for me. Try and tell Mama that.

So, by the time I got up some size she just wasn't talking to me about Daddy. I know she musta missed him some kinda way, 'cause when I would talk about him she'd get this look in her eyes that was saying: *You will bring this man up in my face, won't you? You will reach inside me and try me about this man, won't you? He was a whole lot of things before he was your daddy, Hassalia. He was man of his own, husband to me, and daddy to Esther and Johnnie and ain't no way of knowing who else before he was daddy to you, Hassalia, before you, all of a sudden, were here complicating people's lives and getting compli-*

cated by 'em, before you were even a thought. But you will hurt your Mama like this—the one who feeds you and puts clothes on you and sends you to school. I'm the one you do this way. I'm the one here beating your behind when you won't act right; he's the one off working on the railroad, turning a good dollar as a Pullman porter, and spending it on women you wouldn't want no kinda way for your Mama. But you get all up in my face telling me how you miss this man. Don't, Hassalia, just don't. You don't know what missing is, 'cause you don't know yet what having is. You don't know yet what you got, what you need, what you gon' get and not want, what you gon' get and need to get rid of, what you gon' get and lose, what you gon' be better—or much, much worse—without when it's gone. Get away from me with all of this having, Hassalia, all this holding on to what you think you got, what you think your Daddy was to you, what you think he was to me, what you think he wasn't and never coulda been—oh, no, not your Daddy. I had him, girl, not you. I had him a long time ago. And now I'm full of not having him. And sometimes not having him fills me up to where I'm gonna bust. Other times not having him just makes me empty and mean and bad for everybody, 'specially you. You don't know what having something is, Hassalia, 'til you ain't got it no more, what having somebody is til' you ain't got 'em no more. You're hanging on to your Daddy so you don't have to have what's in front of your eyes: me. Having means not having, Hassalia. You don't have nothing 'til you let go of something else. But you hang on to your Daddy and hang on and hang on. And you don't have him for all of that. I'm the one you got, Hassalia. Look at me.

That's what her eyes would say without her saying it. I'm not gon' say I heard all of that, then. I did hear it, truth to tell, but I didn't know what I was hearing or what to do about any of it, not a blessed thing. About the time I was eight or nine I knew to stop bringing Daddy up to her so much. We weren't seeing him anymore by then. I wanted him to come back. She didn't. I knew I had to stop talking about him so much. I didn't know whether I stopped for me or for her. Now I know it was for me. I wish I'da known how to do it for her then.

Mama never did a whole lot of talking. For sure not to me. I had to figure her out before I opened my mouth, or get my smart mouth slapped. I learned. She would talk to Jim and Ma Rhetta and to Esther. And before he left away she could get real foolish about Johnnie, even after she had to start telling him he was acting too wild and staying out too late and not doing right in school and running around thinking he was cute in front of a lot of white girls their daddies would beat the cute outta him, he didn't watch his step. Mama was kinda two ways about Johnnie. She thought like the rest of us he was cute as the dickens. But when he was 17 and just went away—packed up his Nat King Cole records and left—she knew, like she used to say it, Johnnie gon' find out cute don't pay no rent.

But we never knew what he found out. We didn't hear from Johnnie. I found out later what happened to him, some of it anyway. But Mama didn't know. He was another black man aggravating Mama—like Daddy. I knew Mama was mad at Daddy. Later on I figured out she was mad at Johnnie, too. But I didn't know why she would be until what happened after Ma Rhetta died.

*

I didn't mean to be peeking at anybody. It came from me going up into the attic. Mama said we should leave Ma Rhetta's room pretty much like it was. We took the sickbed stuff out (gave that bedpan back to Dr. Clay), but Mama said to leave the rest of it alone. And she didn't want M'Lady sleeping in there.

M'Lady slept in a little room downstairs off the front hallway, a sewing room is what the white folks who had the house before us called it. The room where M'Lady was was where Johnnie used to sleep, 'cause he wanted a room off to himself, even if it wasn't all that big. I think Mama wanted M'Lady to stay right in that little room, 'cause that way Mama wouldn't start hoping Johnnie would come back. And she didn't want Ma Rhetta's room bothered right then because another empty room in the house woulda made her start thinking about Daddy, how there was still—still—room for him in the house. That old house was big, but until Ma Rhetta was gone it always felt cramped to me, like a lot of us were living on top of each other. I didn't see 'til Ma Rhetta died how much Mama was waiting for Daddy and Johnnie, even if she acted like she forgot about 'em. That was why Esther and Beetsy and me were there, so Mama didn't have to wait by herself. I didn't see all of that then. It just felt like it was a house full of folks that was gonna explode.

Mama didn't want to bother Ma Rhetta's room too much. So we left all her nightgowns in the drawers, and all her dresses in the closet, and her shoes. She didn't wear too much more than housedresses there at the end, but she had clothes from before—some from way back—and Mama said we weren't gon' throw out any of that yet. She would get to it. Told me to leave it alone. Ma Rhetta had so many things: stuff she carried with her from all the places she worked, and things she got from people she knew. She kept a lot of it in her room. Some of it was in the attic. She had pictures of herself and her Mama, Grandma Edna, powder boxes and jewelry boxes and pretty fans and bottles of perfume and little vases and candy dishes and brass candlesticks and two or three old clocks that would chime at the same time when Jim got 'em to working for her, and table lamps and a big floor lamp and lots of combs and jewelry and beaded hairpins. She even had a feather boa constrictor. There were letters and stuff, too, old papers she would look through. Some of it was out on her dresser and some of it was in drawers. The rest of it was in boxes on top of the chifforobe and in the closet.

Mama told me to put it all in some good boxes and take it up to the attic. She didn't want it sitting there collecting dust. She said: "I don't want Ma Rhetta's room looking like this back yard of Jim's." It looked kinda like that already, to me, but Ma Rhetta would dust and clean, or make me do it, and she kept her papers in the kinda order she knew about, even if nobody else did. There was a lot of old stuff Grandma Edna left her, papers and clothes and some old books, and Mama wanted all of that put in the attic. She said she didn't want Ma Rhetta's things just to sit like before, like she wasn't gone, but she didn't want any of it thrown out, either. So, I was s'posed to take it to the attic. Lord knows there wasn't room for it in the basement. Jim had that full up. Mama even said she might rent out Ma Rhetta's room, but none of us believed her.

To get to the attic you went up to the top of the stairs and there was this little door. When you opened it you got into what was like a little tower, hollow and pitch dark. Inside there was a little wooden staircase that went up in a circle to the attic, which went across almost the whole house, front to back. It was big.

Jim didn't keep anything up there. Ma Rhetta didn't allow it, first off, and I knew Mama wouldn't allow it either. It was her house. It was her house long before Ma Rhetta up and died. Ma Rhetta got the house from some white folks Sylvester knew. She didn't leave a will. But there wasn't any doubt everything was all gon' go to Mama anyway—not to Jim or Aunt Fanny or Uncle Grease. Mama was the oldest. So nobody even talked about it when Ma Rhetta died.

Everybody just knew everything was gon' go to Mama. The house wasn't all the way paid for, and Mama was the one making the note payments after Ma Rhetta stopped working. They kinda worked on them together while Ma Rhetta could still work. And even after she stopped, Mama didn't always make them by herself. Daddy helped her some—a lot, he would say when he came to see us. And Jim and Esther helped, too. The bank didn't bother her as long as she made the payments.

But when Ma Rhetta died, the house all of a sudden seemed to everybody like it was Mama's and not anybody else's. Ever since Aunt Fanny left, her and Uncle Grease pretty much kept out of the house and out of Mama's way. We would see Uncle Grease, but he had this funny kinda close feeling of being true to Aunt Fanny, even if he wasn't mad at anybody. I don't think Uncle Grease knew who to be mad at, or why, and that's the biggest reason why what happened to him happened.

Our house was old, but it had a lot of room, and when I would go visit Uncle Grease and Aunt Lyelle and Son-Son and Aunt Fanny at Uncle Grease's house I knew their house was smaller than ours. But I didn't ask myself 'til I got up some size: Why did Aunt Fanny feel better away from our house?

To me, our house was just an old brown house with a big back yard full of junk, and I was so embarrassed by it, what people musta thought, I didn't see how *big* the house was, and what all musta gone on for Ma Rhetta just to get it and have it to turn over to Mama, and why Mama would fight to keep it, even if it did mean putting up with all of Jim's junk in the back yard.

Jim kept on staying there 'cause he wasn't married. Wasn't nobody gon' put him out. Aunt Fanny couldn't come back 'cause she couldn't do for herself and didn't have her mind. Jim was in his right mind, folks could say to themselves, 'cause he was doing for himself. Course, that way of looking at the thing wasn't fair to Aunt Fanny. And Aunt Fanny didn't have anybody to make Ma Rhetta see she had some claim on the place, too. But *would* Ma Rhetta see? It all got back to Sylvester and the soldier, around and around. The two of 'em paying each other back. Looked to me like the men did the wronging. Why were the women the ones hurting each other?

Well, after the funeral, everybody knew the house was Mama's. From the bank to Son-Son, everybody knew that. Uncle Grease was married and had his own house. Not mucha one, but it was his. And you sure couldn't picture Aunt Lyelle living in our house. She got on Mama's nerves too bad. I could see how with Ma Rhetta gone Mama could let Aunt Fanny move back in with us, but I knew she wouldn't. Ma Rhetta and Aunt Fanny fell out too serious about that soldier for Mama to think of it.

But something peculiar started happening to me when I went to moving Ma Rhetta's stuff up to the attic. I'm not just talking about what I found out later—what I saw—on account of going up to the attic. But just by moving anything of Ma Rhetta's without asking her first made me know, all of a sudden, I was in my mother's house. Like I say, it was turning into Mama's house for a long while, even before Ma Rhetta got sick. Back when Ma Rhetta stopped working— she just couldn't stoop over anymore and wash anybody's floors, and her eyes got so bad and her fingers got so crippled up with arthiritis she couldn't sew anymore—was when Mama took over.

But I grew up thinking I lived in *Ma Rhetta's* house. And so did everybody else. That's what they called our house. All the colored and the white, too. I didn't see for a long time what was hurting Ma Rhetta when her time came was, she didn't have her own house any more. She didn't have a man to protect her. She never had one. She got hold of a house on her own, with a little help from Sylvester, and kept it on her own as long as she could. But when she couldn't anymore, here came Mama. Taking over. But did Mama *ask* Ma Rhetta? No. I knew she didn't. Nobody told me. Nobody had to. When Mama told me to take all of Ma Rhetta's stuff up to the attic, it came to me that it was Mama's house and she could do anything she wanted with it. I got scared, really scared. I started thinking serious—not just talking about leaving with Daddy, whenever he decided to come and get me—about leaving that house. I didn't know I already was.

*

One day when I was in the house by myself, a piece of the floor in the attic fell through on me. It wasn't a big hole, and when I fell it didn't make much noise. Esther wasn't home. Beetsy was over at Gregory's. Jim and Mama weren't home either. So nobody but me knew about this piece of floor falling through.

Then I found out across from the main staircase, behind the hall closet, was *another* staircase that went down into the house. The tiny steps went down in a circle. I followed 'em right to the bottom. I lit a match, 'cause it was pitch black in there, and real narrow. They ended up next to the pantry off the kitchen. They didn't go all the way into the basement, so they didn't get into Jim's business down there. I wondered if Jim even knew about 'em. Or did anybody? Nobody ever said anything to me about 'em. How did they get boarded up like that? The white folks who owned the house before us died. That's how Ma Rhetta got hold of it. These folks' chil'ren weren't around when Ma Rhetta moved in, that much I do know. I can remember Ma Rhetta talking about how there was just a real-estate somebody there to give her the keys when it came time for her to move in. So, maybe Ma Rhetta never knew about this little staircase, or Mama and Jim either.

But when I went back up the secret stairs I found the big surprise. This little staircase went right down between Mama's room and Jim's room. The stairs ran next to both rooms, so when you stopped one place on the stairs you were next to Mama's room, and when you went higher you were next to Jim's room. I couldn't see how at first, but I poked along one of the walls and I knocked, and what I heard wasn't solid. It was an echo. I remember thinking, *That's somebody's room behind here*. And when I went down the steps a little bit more I kept knocking against the wall and for a minute it got solid again, and then the sound got hollow again, and I thought, *That's another room*.

I went into Mama's room, which I didn't hardly ever do when she wasn't there. I had to move her dresser from out of the corner, but when I did I knocked on the wall and it sounded hollow in there. It looked to me like it was next to that staircase. Then I went into Jim's room—I never went in there if he wasn't home—and tried the same thing over in his corner, and it sounded hollow in there, too. It was a narrow little secret passage nobody knew about. At least nobody ever said anything to me about it. Like I say, Jim didn't go up into the attic 'cause Ma Rhetta didn't want his stuff up there. So maybe he didn't know about it. The secret staircase did stop on the first floor. It didn't go down into the basement. So, *would* he know? Mama mighta known, but she didn't say anything. Even if she did know, it was all dusty and cobwebby in there, so she didn't go in it. It looked like nobody did.

Did I know right then everything I was gonna find out later? I musta known something. Not everything. But something. 'Cause soon as I figured out where this stairway went and what all it was next to, I knew I wasn't gon' tell anybody about it. I knew I could patch up the hole in the floor myself with some hammer and nails of Jim's. He wouldn't know I used 'em. I would use his tools time by time anyway, so he wouldna cared.

But I didn't want him knowing what I was fixing on doing this time. And I put those boards back so I could work 'em loose easy enough when I wanted to. I hid one of Jim's crowbars in the attic to do it.

It was gon' be my secret. Even if Mama or Jim or somebody else went up to the attic, the way I fixed those boards they weren't gon' fall through. I put my weight on 'em, jumping up and down, and they held fine. Unless somebody was looking for this staircase nobody was gon' find it, and nobody could be looking for it unless they already knew it was there.

The other thing I knew right off was that I was gon' go onto that staircase real quiet and listen to see if I could hear anything in Mama's room or Jim's. I don't know to this day what called me to do such a thing. But I wanted to know if I could be quiet enough to do it without them hearing me. And I wanted to know if I could hear what was going on in their room, Mama or Jim, even if it wasn't anything but them snoring.

*

Mama didn't keep comp'ny, not since Daddy left. I never saw her with any man. When women would come over and sit and talk about menfolks, Mama had a whole lot to say. But then they'd say, "Ruby, girl, when you gon' go on out there and do something for yourself?" They wouldn't say anything about Daddy, but they were signifying, saying...*like Izell's doing for himself?* without saying it right out. Mama would laugh and say, "Hmpf! Do you know a man who's worth more than the trouble he gives? If you do, why aren't you after him yourself?" Even the ones who were married would laugh at that. If I was in the room she'd say,

"Hassalia, go on out to the kitchen and help Ma Rhetta with supper," or "Hassalia, run down to the store for me." She'd give me some money and I'd be gone. I figured that was when she musta talked the worst about Daddy. I guess she didn't see any use in letting me hear it, 'cause I'da just raised sand over it and she wasn't gon' change her feelings to suit me anyway, so why sit up and argue with a chile? I don't know what she thought, truthfully, but she musta talked about Daddy when I wasn't there, and a lot of what she said was bad, I know, 'cause a lot of what she said about him to my face was bad.

∗

Jim would see women away from the house. Where they lived, or in some of those kinda houses, too. He wouldn't bring 'em in front of Ma Rhetta. Ma Rhetta could talk Christian good as the next person, and read her Bible at you, too. Jim wouldna tangled with Ma Rhetta about nothing like that. I can remember Sting Ray and a bunch of other men one time asking Jim if he wanted to get married. All he did was suck a little bit deeper on his toothpick and say, "What I want to get married for?" and looked dead at whoever asked him. Nobody knew what to say when he said that.

∗

I kept my secret about the staircase. I finished putting Ma Rhetta's stuff up in the attic. Mama went into Ma Rhetta's room and looked around and told me a couple more things she wanted me to take up there. Then I was through.

Come daytime, when Mama and Esther and Jim would be out working, and I had the house to myself—Beetsy would be down at Uncle Grease's playing with Son-Son—

107

I would work loose those boards and slip on down that staircase and knock on those walls just to see what I could hear, what kinda echo I would get back.

I knew I could hear a lot, but I couldn't see anything! I drilled a little hole in Mama's room first, to see if I could. It was next to the little table where she kept her telephone, the kinda place on the wall where you look but don't see. When she was looking at that part of the wall, all she'd be looking for was the telephone, and that's all she'd see. It was just a little eyehole for one eye, but it was big enough for me to see into her room.

After I knocked around a while in Jim's room I figured out how to run a hole right over the molding at the top of his room, near the corner where the two pieces of molding came together. It was high up, so I could see pretty near the whole room—the door, the bed, the rug, the closet. Jim didn't have much in there but a chest of drawers and a little desk over in the corner where he did some of his paperwork for his business.

Some people used to think Jim was a stupid nigger trash man who wouldna had sense enough to keep business records. But when he got to pulling out records on 'em, they thought one more time. Jim wasn't a fool. He kept books. He would keep accounts and have folks sign the invoice when he sold 'em something and a release when he bought something from 'em—I mean something like a big expensive oak table or a next door to brand new Amana freezer or a 21" Zenith or a sharp set of hubcaps off of somebody's '53 Merc. That kinda stuff Jim would write down. He didn't just do it with a handshake. That's why people dealt careful with him.

I knew I was gon' look and see what both of 'em were doing. I felt funny about it. I would get all tight in my stomach and nervous when I was gon' do it, like I had to go to the bathroom. The first time was dead in the night. I got outta bed and went up toward the attic in my bare feet. With that crowbar I kept in my room I loosed the boards real quiet and crept down the secret stairs. I had a flashlight. When I looked down into Jim's room there was enough light coming in the window from the street light outside so I could see him lying there sleeping. He was flat on his back, with his mouth half open. He wasn't snoring, but he looked like he should be. He had a blanket over him, so I couldn't see whether he was in his underwear or not. Then I went on a little bit further down the stairs 'til I was next to the little hole I cut in the wall of Mama's room. I put a piece of tape across from it on the staircase so I could find it. I looked in there and saw Mama on her bed, sleeping, with her back to me. She had a clock ticking in there, like the ones in Ma Rhetta's room, but it was funny how in the daytime when I was in Mama's room I didn't pay it any attention. I could hear it real good right then, though, and at first I wondered how she slept through it. I guess she was used to it and musta slept deep.

I swear before God I didn't know what I was doing or why I would want to peek at anybody. The thing was, right then—when I was still a chile and next door to a woman, but not a woman yet—I thought I was in the right. I thought it was all right for me to look at folks who didn't know I was looking at 'em. Everybody in that house was always looking at me and telling me what to wear and where to go and not go and how to look and what to say and not to talk back. I wasn't a chile. But they were still treating me like one.

I knew there was *something* going on in that house. I could tell by the way people looked at me before Ma Rhetta died when they would ask me how she was doing and how was Mama and how was Esther. Folks didn't ask much about how Jim was. They'd most likely ask, menfolks in particular, what Jim was doing. "Jim listening to the game this afternoon?" "Jim out of town today?" "Tell Jim I'll be around to see him, Has, I got some lumber I want him to try and sell for me."

But their eyes said: *Goodness, Hassalia, don't you know yet what all is happening in your house? You're the baby, so I guess maybe you don't.*

I could see 'em thinking I was some kinda fool, and in my mind I was screaming back at em: *What are y'all laughing at me for? What do y'all know that I don't? I know you think I'm crazy 'cause I dress like a boy and 'cause my Uncle's a junk man and my Mama just thinks about how bad my Daddy's treated her and it looks like he's never gon' come back, and y'all can tell how bad I want him to come back, but you think if I knew more about him I wouldn't be so quick to want him back. But I don't care what y'all say. I do want my Daddy to come back and take me out of here away from all of y'all.*

And so what if my Uncle Jim is a junk man? Y'all come to him one time or another when you need something cheap and want to pay next to nothing for it and you too shamefaced to ask white folks. And so what if Ma Rhetta had four chil'ren and no husband? And so what if my Mama can't help it how she stays mad at my Daddy? It doesn't mean my Mama doesn't have feelings for me. And so what if my sister Esther had Sting Ray's baby and he isn't anywhere around half the time, and they're just some kinda married and not married for real with a house and all? And so what if my brother Johnnie lit out of here when he was 17 to be somebody and isn't anybody at all now, anywhere? And so what if my Aunt Fanny lost some of her mind and talks out of her head sometimes and plays with Son-Son like the two of 'em are related mama to chile or man to woman? And so what if my Uncle Grease and Aunt Lyelle together are so skinny you couldn't get 'em to weigh much more than 200 pounds between 'em, and so quiet you hardly know they said something even when they did? So what if I don't look to you like I come from anything but junk and a family that buys and sells junk—old, nasty things white and colored both throw out and don't want any more? Y'all think we're junk, too. But we're not junk.

I would think like that a lot. After Ma Rhetta died it got worse. It felt like everybody colored in Crawley was waiting to see what we were gon' do next. What respect did they have for Ma Rhetta, or what we were feeling, was what I wanted to know. I couldn't tell. I wasn't even sure who to ask. Reverend Jonas preached Ma Rhetta's funeral, but he wouldna told us anyway. He was just another one of the colored who looked at us like we were crazy. I know 'cause when Ma Rhetta got down sick he would come by to see how she was doing. Once a month, Monday after first Sunday, he would bring the little tray and the grape juice and the crackers and give her communion, before she got so she didn't know what was happening to her anymore. And after he would finish he couldn't wait to get out of there, away from Ma Rhetta and all of us. He thought we were all crazy, just like everybody else did.

The only white folks who ever came to our house were the doctor, the insurance man and the paper boy. I wouldn't even let my white friend, Roy, come inside the house. He would ask me about things Jim had in the yard and sometimes I'd take him stuff. But I didn't want him coming in there. There were enough other places for us to go. I thought if he ever told his mama and daddy he was inside our house they'da told him he couldn't have anything to do with me any more. When he'd come by to get me he'd just whistle from the street or knock on the back door and we'd get in the wind. We didn't need to talk. We were just gone. I liked me some tall, skinny, sweet ol', slow talking, next to no talking Roy Sharkey, don't ask me to lie, and I didn't want him to go away.

*

I was a stranger in my own house. I started slipping around
like some slick detective or sheriff trying to catch Richard
Conte or Jack Palance doing something they weren't s'posed
to be doing. I was either Robert Mitchum or Randolph
Scott.

I was sly. I hid. I didn't know I was gonna be like that, I
just was.

*

I liked to get up early. Me and Roy would go fishing. We'd
make us a raft and float in the middle of the day when it got
warm. I used to stay out all day. I wasn't thinking about
going to college. I didn't know where money from it was
coming from. Roy was going for sure. I knew that. For now
he was waiting out and working for a year in his daddy's
hardware store, but next year he was going away to school.

I was good with tools and there was this auto shop out
on the highway that let me work there after school. I started
out slow, changing spark plugs and pumping gas, and
working in the car wash they had there, too. Then after I got
out of school they let me go to taking apart engines. Jim
talked to 'em so they'd let me do it. The white man didn't
care if I was a girl or not, he said, long as I didn't mind
working around a lot of engines and noise and bad-talking
men. I was thinking about doing it permanent.

Before I started working there I would make money
raking leaves and cutting lawns and helping Jim when he'd
let me. And I was taking auto shop in school. I was the only
girl. I wanted to and the principal told Mama it was all right
with him as long as none of the other parents complained.
None of 'em did, not then. The teacher, Mr. Bailey, said I
was good at it. The white boys in the class teased me when

I started, but after a while they started to pay attention when I would ask a question, 'cause I was usually on the way to figuring out what the teacher was gonna say next. Fixing cars is like anything else, it helps if you have a feeling for it. I could work with tools. Hanging around all those broken parts Jim had in the back yard, I could pick up anything and figure out how it was s'posed to go. Jim was better than I was, but if he got behind he would tell me to take over some stuff that he was working on down in the basement. He would give me some of the money he made off of what he sold. That's how when I got to metal shop and then auto shop in school, I could do stuff pretty good. I liked tools, and grease and dirt didn't bother me, the way it woulda most girls.

So I was thinking about taking this job permanent at the auto repair shop. The white man's son was filling in, doing some light stuff for a while, but the next semester he was going away to school, and the man said I could try it.

So I was thinking about the job and trying not to think about Ma Rhetta being gone, because what good did that do? I would be away from the house a lot, sometimes all day. Sometimes me and Roy would take the train into Chicago for the whole day and go to the movies and walk around by Lake Michigan and the Art Institute and stuff. We would eat all kinda food we wanted, and just fool around. People would look at us, a white boy and a colored girl in overhalls laughing and talking and having a good time all over the street, but we didn't care. We just did it and came on back to Crawley. Roy had a girlfriend, but her mama and daddy never woulda let her run around all day with Roy like that, the way me and him could. Roy told his folks we were good friends, and nothing was gon' happen that shouldna.

*

One night I went to the kitchen to get some peanut butter and jelly and a glass of milk. When I came back up the stairs I saw the end of Mama's housecoat going into Jim's room. The door shut right behind it. I knew what I saw. I got my flashlight, tipped quiet up the stairs to the attic and pulled loose the floorboards. I didn't need a crowbar. I left 'em loose from the last time. I knew nobody was going up in the attic any more unless it was me. When I got on the secret stairs I already knew how quiet I had to be. It was like what I did before, when I first found out about them, was all practice. I got to the hole where I could see into Jim's room. I didn't look. I just listened.

"She the Mama of you don't mean she your Mama." That was Jim.

"And don't talk about a Daddy." That was Mama.

"No? Don't talk about a Daddy?"

They got quiet.

"Uhm."

"We got us a Daddy, you know that, girl."

"Uhm."

"We got us a Daddy?"

"Uhm, yeah, we got us a Daddy."

"Daddy got what we need?"

"Yeah, Daddy got what we need."

"Daddy got what we want?"

"Yes, Lawd, Daddy got what we want."

"You got what Daddy want?"

"Yeah, I got what Daddy want."

"Got what Daddy need?"

"Yeah, I got what Daddy need."

"What's Daddy got to do to get what Daddy got to have?"

"Daddy don't have to do nothing."

"He got it?"

"Yes, yes, you got it, Daddy."

They got quiet again. I couldn't look through the hole. I heard them making noises, lips and tongues, and Mama would moan, "Yes Daddy, yes Daddy, yes Daddy," but I couldn't hear Jim say anything. I couldn't stand it any more, so I got out of there, quiet, so they wouldn't hear me.

I put the boards back slow and easy. After that, all I was thinking about right that second was getting back to my room before Mama came out of there. I didn't think she was coming out soon, but I didn't want her to catch me out of bed.

In my room I got back into bed before I thought about anything. I kept it all stone out of my mind until I was in bed curled up real tight. I put my arms around myself and closed my eyes. Then I started to cry.

I was so mad at Mama I didn't know what to do. I thought if Daddy ever found out what she doing he'd beat up on her and Jim. I wanted my Daddy to see this mess.

Then I wondered what Ma Rhetta would say if she knew what was going on in her house. Was it going on before she died? I couldn't tell from what the two of 'em said. Mama missed Daddy and stayed mad at Daddy. I just didn't know how bad. Jim didn't have anybody. Never had a woman he would bring to meet Ma Rhetta anyway. I never heard Ma Rhetta ask him about getting married. From when I was a chile seemed like to me he just wasn't gon' get married. He was just Jim.

But how could him and Mama do that? Jim was Mama's brother. He was my uncle. How could they be acting nasty like that with each other? I knew what I heard. They musta been doing it before. But when? I never saw 'em, never heard 'em before.

I trembled.

PART FOUR

ESTHER, 1957

*TSHEMBE: Race is a device—no more,
no less. It explains nothing at all...And
it is pointless to pretend that it doesn't
exist—merely because it is a lie.*

—Lorraine Hansberry
Les Blancs

THE NEXT TIME WAS IN BROAD DAYLIGHT. It was a couple of days later, a Saturday afternoon, and Mama was working late at her white folks'. I didn't know where Beetsy was. M'Lady was there, but she was always there. It didn't matter. Mama and me saw after her in her room, or maybe we'd wheel her in her wheelchair out on the back porch and let her sit in the sun and look at all that junk. She just looked. She never said anything. Her eyes would hardly blink.

I was supposed to be working at the auto shop all day. I went there that morning. But not too long after I got there Mr. Chandler said, "Has, let me see you in·the office." I finished filling somebody's car with gas and Rusty took over for me at the pump. I went into the office and sat down. I was wearing grease monkey coveralls like I was s'posed to do and I had on my red baseball cap, which I took off before I sat down. I put it in my back pocket. I started to play with Peggy, the big pretty collie dog Mr. Chandler kept around there. She was a beautiful thing, and I liked her. Everybody did. She stayed out of the way. Her coat would get all dirty, and Mr. Chandler's kids had to bathe her all the time. Clean off the oil along with the dirt. Said he wasn't gon' stop bringing her down to the shop when she kept everybody such good comp'ny and didn't cause any trouble.

I was sitting there playing with Peggy while Mr. Chandler was on the phone. When he got off he said, nice and easy,

"Here, Has, have one." And he threw me his pack of Pall Malls. I took one out and lit it up. I figured this was gonna be some kind of a long talk, but I didn't know about what. The morning wasn't busy yet, but it would be soon.

"Has, you're a real good worker here. What you're doing here in this station and in this body shop and in the car wash and all—you haven't hit the coffee shop yet, but I'll bet you could do that fine, too—well, it's real good, Has."

"Thanks, Mr. Chandler. I like working around here, being around cars and stuff, and the guys. I just like it."

"I see you do, Has. I see you do." He waited. "But not everybody, Has, looks at this thing the way you and I do."

"No?"

"No."

"What do you mean?

"Well, some folks say, you being a girl and all, it isn't right, working in a big dirty garage with a lot of men hanging around using all kinds of language and telling who knows what kind of stories. Lot of rough talk."

"But you know that kinda stuff doesn't bother me. And I don't get with 'em. The guys get to talking dirty with a customer while he's waiting for his car to get fixed, I'll go over to the car wash and find something to do. Or I'll go out and help load tires to go for burning, you know?"

"I know, Has, I know. And I know you don't wait for them to tell you stories. But you're not always gonna be able to get out of the way of those stories if you're gonna work here. And there's a lot of men come in here from all over town, some of them bigshots, you know that, and my customers just don't feel it's right having a girl in the shop. And I'm beginning to think they're right, Has, I really am."

I couldn't understand what he was saying. "But Mr. Chandler, you said you like my work. Some of *them* say they like my work—Mr. Bascomb told you how fast I fixed his carburetor last week. And I'm starting to do good body work—fenders, bumpers, doors. And I can spray paint 'em good, too. I get the color matches right. I'm real careful, you know I am."

"Yes, Has, you are. You do good work. But a girl like you doesn't wanna be doing work like this. One day you're gonna come in here and tell me you're gonna be getting married, and you know no man's gonna want you to work in a place like this."

"Mr. Chandler, I told you I'm not thinking about marrying anybody right now. I want to learn this."

"Has, my customers just aren't gonna stand for having a girl in here any longer. It was a crazy idea from the start. I let you and Rusty talk me into it. I shouldna done it in the first place."

"Mr. Chandler, wait a minute. It's because I'm a Negro, isn't it?"

"Has, no. No. That has no bearing. Put that out of your mind."

"These white men coming in here with their cars, or these white ladies coming in with their station wagons full of kids, they called you up, didn't they, and told you they don't want me pumping their gas or vacuuming inside their cars before they get washed or going in their trunks to check their spares, didn't they? They don't want somebody colored doing that, do they?"

"Has, look, you can go other places and do this. You can go into the city if you want. There might be some stations in there that would let you. But not out here."

"Some colored gas station, is that what you mean? There aren't many, Mr. Chandler. There aren't many in Chicago at all. I checked. Jim, my uncle, he checked, too. White people own 'em all. If colored are working there, there are plenty of other colored right in their neighborhood who want the job if one comes open. They don't need a colored girl from some country town coming in there for a job. I want to work here, Mr. Chandler, right here in Crawley. This is where I grew up. I went to school here, with Rusty and everybody else. Yeah, I'm a girl, but I like this kinda work and I can do it. But you don't want a colored girl in here, isn't that right?"

"I'm sorry you're looking at this thing that way, Has. You're a nice girl. You can do a lot of things besides getting yourself dirty all day doing this kind of work."

"Can I, Mr. Chandler? Can I? Doing what? Could I be a tender over at the swimming pool this past summer? No, Mr. Chandler, I couldn't. Why? Because they just started letting us swim in the pool a couple of years ago. You know they don't want any of us tending it. I know enough about plumbing, I know enough about pipes to learn what to do. But they won't let me. And they sure weren't going to let me be a lifeguard, putting my black hands on their little white children, even if they were drowning.

"Could I go downtown and sell in one of the stores? Even if I did put on a dress, will they let a colored girl do it, Mr. Chandler? No. They won't even let me be a box boy—or box girl—in the A&P. Never mind being a checkout clerk.

"I can clean houses, Mr. Chandler. That's what white folks will let me do. Clean their house, wearing a white uniform, like my mother and my sister do. Scrub floors on their knees. And some of these folks will let me take care of their kids when I get to be fifty. For now, I can go work at the electrical plant on the night shift sticking wires into coffee pots and toasters, and, when I get real good, a hi-fi. For $2.75 an hour. They won't let a girl be a janitor at the courthouse. I know, 'cause I asked Mr. Sullivan. He already works there. They told him the work was too heavy for a girl. You want me in a flower shop instead of an auto shop, 'cause that's better for a girl, but they won't let me in the flower shop. Here I'm in the grease and the grime. I like it. Who does it hurt? I don't have any place else to go right now that's gonna pay me any money. How come I can't work here?"

He stood up. "Has, I'm sorry. There isn't anything I can do about this."

I looked at him. Then I said, "If you can't do anything about it, why are you sorry?"

"Has, you're a girl."

"A colored girl."

"A girl. And girls just can't do this kinda work. I wouldn't let a white girl do it."

"A white girl wouldn't want to, Mr. Chandler. She'd get some thing else to do. A teller at the bank, an usher at the show. Or sell ribbons at the dime store. They wouldn't let my aunt sell ribbons out front at the five and dime, Mr. Chandler, and they won't let me, either. They still won't."

"Has, this just isn't gonna work. Today's your last day. I'm sorry."

I got up out of the chair and headed for the door. I was crying and I knew he saw me crying, but I didn't care. I just told him straight out. "You don't want me here, Mr. Chandler. Why don't you just say it?"

He didn't say anything. I turned around and walked out of the office.

I went to my locker and changed out of my coveralls. Rusty came over to me.

"You knew, didn't you?"

"Yeah, Has, I knew. He told me he was gonna do it. I know it's not right, Has. I know it's not. I told him I wished he hadna hired you like he did, and got you all hoping and everything."

"You don't want me here, either?"

"It's not like that, Has. It just wouldn't work out. Some people already started complaining. My Dad didn't know what else to do."

"Get out of my way, Rusty."

"Has, don't feel like that. We had a lot of good times. You can play basketball like nobody's business, Has. Remember how I would be center and you guard? I'd pass and you'd shoot. Remember, Has?"

"In a minute you and your Daddy are gonna be telling me to be a basketball player, Rusty. You want me to be anywhere except working here in this damn garage. You go to hell, Rusty."

I left there and just started walking. The gas station was out on the highway, about a mile from the house. But I didn't feel like going straight home. I walked out to the lake and back, ten miles. I cried a lot at first. And I talked to Daddy.

I felt so sad and so mad. Ma Rhetta was gone. Mama and Jim were acting up. Esther never did have good sense, and that crazy Sting Ray was back around somewhere. He wasn't in Crawley yet, but he was around. He was calling up Esther and she was getting all excited, talking about the two of 'em taking Beetsy and going off together. And now I lost my job to white folks. My whole house was falling apart, seemed like, and there wasn't anything I could do to make it stand up.

It was after 3 o'clock when I got home. I didn't eat anywhere, but I still wasn't hungry. I came in the back door, in the kitchen. I was being more quiet than I knew I was being. I sat down at the kitchen table. Didn't even get a drink of water. Just sat.

First off, I just thought I heard something. I wasn't sure there was anything there at all. Then I heard something that wasn't new—it was old; I heard it before—but it was something I didn't really hear, didn't really pay the right attention to, 'til right then.

I still didn't know right off what it was. It took some figuring. There I was, at the kitchen table, thinking maybe a cup of Hershey cocoa would make me feel better. Then I heard this noise, low, coming from way, way back in somebody's throat. It came out one little noise after another, not fast, not slow, but like there wasn't any help for it, it was coming *out*: "Uhhhhh hhhh, uhhhhhhhhhhhh, uhhhhhhhhhhh." Somewhere between a moan and a cry. Right then, when I heard it, low as it was, I couldna told you whether it was man or woman, young or old—or even if it was *somebody*. Coulda been a cat; coulda been the mouse the cat caught; coulda been a dog happy as could be with a bone—or trying, slowlike, to cough the bone up before it tore his throat wide open or choked him to death. Whoever it was or whatever it was, I couldna told you right then if they wanted the noise to stop or to keep on.

My mind went hunting before my body did. I listened. Didn't even worry right off where it was coming from. First thing I wondered, is it young or old? Beetsy or M'Lady? M'Lady had her little room right down the hallway from the kitchen, and if it had been coming from there I coulda told. So, I told myself it wasn't her. Then it came to me it mighta been Beetsy. Sometimes she would crawl up somewhere in some corner and sing to one of her little ol ' raggedy dolls, or lay down on that little rug she took a nap on at kindergarten that she was supposed to leave at school but kept sneaking home when the teacher wasn't looking. She loved that thing. It wasn't anything but a little ol' pallet (it wasn't straw; it was a rug, but it wasn't a real deep rug) that me and Mama marched Esther down to the dime store to buy when Beetsy started kindergarten. Esther couldn't get it into her mind that little children in school needed a nap. She didn't remember taking naps when she was in school. We told her they did now and Beetsy needed a rug like the rest of 'em.

Beetsy got so crazy about this rug she was bringing it home after school and taking naps on it in the evening, falling to sleep before me or Mama or somebody would pick her up and carry her upstairs and put her to bed in Esther's room. And she'd try her best to sneak the thing home on Friday so she could take naps on it on Saturday and Sunday. We'd find her curled up on her little rug in a corner somewhere in the house, with her little lunch box next to her and peanut butter and jelly in the corners of her mouth. Between that rug and that lunch box and the sandwiches me or Mama or Ma Rhetta would put in it, we got the chile crazy about going to school. She would bring school home with her. She would sit on the little rug and take rides on it in her mind, floating out the window and all over Crawley and everywhere else. We would ask her where she was going, and she'd say, "I'm gon' catch up with Granddaddy on one of his trains. I'm gon' fly right by the window and look inside and say, 'Hi, Granddaddy Izell! How you doing in there? Your train ain't going fast enough for me today.'" And she'd bust up laughing. Or she'd fly down to Uncle Grease and Aunt Lyelle's house to see them and Aunt Fanny. Or when we'd tell her Aunt Fanny was away for a while—in the state place, for folks who weren't right in the head, but we wouldn't tell her that—she'd say she was going to find Aunt Fanny, and we'd say to tell Aunt Fanny we all said Hi. Beetsy kept on with that rug, even though she was in the first grade now, and there kids didn't take naps any more.

So right then I started thinking, if it wasn't M'Lady (and I didn't think it was) then it mighta been Beetsy flying somewhere on her rug. It didn't sound like Mama or Jim or Esther were home. Maybe they went somewhere and left Beetsy asleep on the rug, 'cause they didn't want to carry her with 'em. She coulda been in M'Lady's room talking to her, but, like I say, if the sound was coming from there I coulda told from the kitchen. It wasn't coming from there. Something about this sound told me it wasn't Beetsy. But to make sure I had to go and see.

I went down to the hallway and stuck my head in M'Lady's room. Sure enough, she was just sitting in her wheelchair staring out her window. I didn't bother her. She could get back and forth to the bathroom by herself, and when she was hungry she could wheel on into the kitchen and find herself something to eat if she wanted to. You didn't worry about her. She was so quiet, even when you couldn't see her you could feel her, and you'd go check on her. Other times she'd be right in the same room with you and you'd completely forget her.

I didn't see Beetsy in there, so I thought she might be lying on her rug somewhere in the house making that noise.

I heard it again, and that time I could tell it was coming from upstairs. It got shorter: "Uuh, uuh, uuh." I didn't want to think what it was. I thought what it was, but I didn't want to. If it was Mama again, she didn't sound like the last time, or like she ever sounded to me before. I went on up the stairs, real, real quiet.

It was from down the hall. Jim's room. There was nothing for me to do but go up to the entrance to the attic and down into the secret stairs to see if I could see what was going on. I remember thinking maybe we were all going crazy, me included. Even if Jim was doing whatever he was in his room, what was I doing slipping around like I was, looking at folks when they didn't know I was looking? Out at the lake in the summertime sometimes me and Roy would follow folks and watch 'em swimming naked and kissing and even going all the way. I felt funny doing it but I didn't feel like I was bad. I wanted to see, but I wasn't gon' tell on anybody. Roy neither. We never did. Course we never did 'cause folks woulda known we were peeking when we shouldna been.

But what I was feeling right then while I was climbing down those secret stairs to look into Jim's room wasn't the same as me and Roy peeking at somebody out at the lake.

When I was creeping up on Jim like I was, all I could think about was Ma Rhetta. I think after I heard Jim and Mama making those sounds, in my head I started hearing the same sounds from Ma Rhetta and Sylvester. They couldna been the same. But Ma Rhetta and Sylvester musta sounded like somebody or something when they snuck and saw each other, took off their clothes and started feeling on each other like a man and a woman do. What did they sound like? What were they thinking? Did they know they were making Aunt Fanny? Did Ma Rhetta and that conjure man know they were making Mama? Did her and Mr. Brown know they were making Jim? Who made Uncle Grease with Ma Rhetta, and what did it sound like? I bet none of 'em sounded the same.

What did Mama and Daddy Izell sound like when they were making Esther and then Johnnie and then me? Did Jim and Mama know what they were making when they made the sound they did? What was going on in Jim's room right now? Besides noise, what was getting made?

What I saw when I got to where I could look down into Jim's room got burned into my head because the exact same minute I put my eye up to the peephole the sound— "uuuhhhhhh"—came out again. It was Esther. She was bent way over. Jim was behind her, standing up. His thing was up in her pussy, not in her behind, but the way she was moaning at first I thought it was. I don't think he was hurting her as much as he was surprising her. Her legs were spread wide and I could see her mouth open and dribbling all over the pillow she had under her face. Jim had his eyes closed like he was concentrating. And Esther was steady moaning. I wondered did she sound like this when her and Sting Ray made Beetsy.

I got out of there as fast as I could. I just couldn't look at that. I didn't know what that fool Esther thought she was doing. Or did she even know? What kinda desperator did she have to be to do something like that? Or what kinda spell was Jim working on folks—her and Mama—to make 'em do that?

I did a funny thing. I didn't go to my room, I didn't go back to the kitchen. I almost got there and then I stopped in front of M'Lady's room. It was near about the end of the day, and the sun was falling fast, shining in her window. And she was sitting there looking at it shine through the window and onto her wall. It was almost down, almost through. I went in there and sat down on the floor next to her in her wheelchair, and put my head down on her lap and cried and cried and cried. In the middle of all that crying I started talking. I knew M'Lady never seemed like she heard anything anybody said. But I talked anyway.

"What's happening to everybody, M'Lady? If Ma Rhetta was here none of this would be going on. Have folks lost their minds? Everything everybody ever said about this family must be true. Nobody in this house cares who's the daddy of who. Long as there's a mama left to take care of the baby, folks don't care what they make or who they make it with. That's how Mama and Daddy Izell made me, M'Lady. They weren't thinking about me when they made me, they were thinking about *them*. And that's why my Daddy doesn't wanna come back here and look at me, M'Lady. He's shamefaced, 'cause he knows he didn't care anyway. He didn't. He didn't really want a baby girl—me— when he made me. He was through. He had Esther and Johnnie. At least he stayed here with them for a while. But I came along and he decided that was enough making babies and he was gon' go away and make something else now, and stay away. Never mind Mama. Never mind the rest of us. And now all of 'em maybe making babies and they don't care either. How come they can't let this world be without sticking their things inside each other? Never mind who the daddy and mama are, never mind what the baby looks like or feels like or wants. If you're the Mama you gotta stay 'cause somebody's gotta feed the baby if it's not gonna die. But if you're the daddy you don't have to stay. And the mama gets mad but she's still wishing the daddy was there, wishing she didn't have the baby all alone. And folks don't wanna stop doing what they do until they hurt more folks like they've been hurt. Nobody cares, M'Lady. And I'm not gonna care either. You watch. I'm gonna take off all o' my clothes some time and jump into bed with some man and let him stick his thing in me and I'm gonna moan and cry and carry on like it feels good and he's still not gonna stay, and I'm gonna have a baby after that and that man's gonna stay just long enough to get one look at what we made. And then he'll be long gone, M'Lady. He's not gon' be wishing for me or thinking about me or thinking about any baby, 'cause the baby's made, M'Lady, and he doesn't need a woman hanging around his neck after that 'til he feels like making another baby. She's always gon' see him in that baby's eyes and he doesn't want that. He thinks it's him down there between his legs. That's why one baby doesn't mean any more than another to any of 'em. Well, they aren't touching me 'til I'm good and ready , M'Lady, not a one of 'em. Oh, Ma Rhetta, if you could see *today*. If you could *see*." I kept on crying there on M'Lady's lap, soaking her housecoat.

Like I say, M'Lady didn't ever talk. When she was hungry she could tell us with her hands. And most of the time she made sounds to herself like we weren't even there. Sometimes we would be watching TV and she would get to making sounds in her throat and one of us would have to go over to her and just put our hand, real gentle, over her mouth. And she'd stop. You didn't have to do more than that.

After I finished talking and was still there crying she started making a sound in her throat. I didn't know what it was. It was like all of her sounds. It was just there. I didn't think about her really hearing me. I was crying. She made a sound. We both were making sounds.

But then: "Hush, child." It was M'Lady. I heard it, but I still didn't stop crying completely 'cause I didn't hear it all the way.

Then I heard: "Hush, now, hush. Your Mama's coming home to you. She's not gonna leave a pretty little girl all alone. And you can't be pretty with all of those tears making your eyes red and swollen. Calm yourself, daughter, calm yourself." She called me "daughter", like Ma Rhetta did. But she said it real proper. Nice, but not exactly like Ma Rhetta woulda. She stroked my head real slow. I couldn't tell if she knew what she was feeling, if she ever felt a colored girl's short, nappy hair before, with the little bit of Dixie Peach I put on it that morning coming off on her fingers. But she didn't stop, not all the way into the sun going down and me and her sitting there together in the beginning of the dark. She called me "daughter". And there I was, "her" chile. Nobody's chile was what I felt like.

*

Ruby. "If there was an easy way, Hassalia, I woulda took the easy way. There ain't nar'un. Don't let nobody tell you any different. I was my Mama's chile all my life. I wasn't my daddy's chile, 'cause he wasn't there. The way you go on like you do about missing your daddy, Hassalia, I'm not sure you know what missing is. You act like you're missing something you had, and the truth is you didn't have your daddy, not like a young girl shoulda. It pains me to tell you straight out like that, but that's the Lord's truth. I know you think I don't mean your daddy any good, and would never say any good about him. I would, Hassalia, I would. If I could see it I would. But your daddy didn't wanna be the

---

131

daddy of his children all the way out, 'til the children got grown. Johnnie thought he could make himself into Nat King Cole or Sam Cooke or somebody, but he's really looking for his daddy, Hassalia. And I'm gon' tell you something, girl: he ain't found him. Not Izell or Nat King Cole. Johnnie's gonna have to be his own daddy. I hope he's somewhere doing that, but truth to tell I don't think so. I don't see how you can be daddy to your own self.

"I know, 'cause I didn't have a daddy. Ma Rhetta told me about my daddy. I know she told you something about him before she died, some time or other. But she didn't tell you what I did for a daddy, did she? She couldna told you that, because she didn't know. Just like I don't know what you do for a daddy with Izell gone like he been gone for so long now. But I do know you make out like your mama's cruel and never loved your daddy and probably doesn't love you. But love's not like that, Hassalia. You think I don't have eyes, chile? You think I don't see how you look when anybody talks about their daddy? You miss your daddy, and you're not sure he loved you. Well, girl, what am I s'posed to tell you? I'm not sure, either.

"Ma Rhetta wasn't easy, Hassalia. Coming up like we did, me and her and Jim, before Fanny came along, it was just the three of us. And me and Jim were looking to her, but you think she could do it all? Unh-unh, honey. Nobody can do it all. You can only tell your children so much about a daddy who's not there. And me and Jim didn't have the *same* daddy. So how were we s'posed to keep from thinking maybe Ma Rhetta liked one of us better than the other counta she liked one of our daddies better than the other? Or did she hate 'em both, and hate us 'cause the daddies didn't stay?

"I don't think she knew who she loved or what she loved. She kinda loved her own self to make sure she got some loving and that made her reach out like she did to Sylvester.

I know she told you about all of that. She had more to tell you, Hassalia, but she didn't know how. She couldna done it. I know 'cause it took her long enough to see what all she was doing and what the church folks was saying about her behind her back. Not that they didn't say it to her face, too. They did. That was what made it so hard on all of us. You didn't know what they were saying behind your back. And it was probably worse than what they were saying to your face. Me and Jim grew up with all o' that, Hassalia. We didn't ever know what people were saying about our Mama.

"Me and Jim don't know anybody better than we know each other, that's the truth. He was the one *there*. Ma Rhetta wasn't the one for sure. She raised us up, Hassalia, but she couldn't stop folks from talking. 'Cause a lot of what folks were saying was true. Just like a lot of what I tell you about your daddy—like when I tell you he oughta sent more money than he did, and shouldna chased women like he did—that's true, too, even if you don't wanna hear it. Girl, if I went on about my daddy the way you go on about yours, I 'd turn him into a Baptist preacher in my mind. But that's not what he was. He was some kinda conjure man, but he didn't bring any peace like the pain he left. And he left fast, honey, let me tell you. Ma Rhetta told me more than one time. And wherever he is now, heaven or hell or in between, I'll bet you he's still running. A man like that won't slow down for God if God doesn't do the slowing.

"And your daddy's the same way. Don't fool yourself, girl. Only thing that man loves better than the road is a lie. The road's where he learned so many lies to come back and tell me, when he did feel like coming back. Didn't matter I was here scrubbing floors, and doing the best I could for *his* children. And when Ma Rhetta got like she couldn't work like she used to, what was I gonna do, put her in the street? Your daddy knew that. He knew Ma Rhetta didn't have a man to take care of her proper, never did have one. Not proper. 'Cause another man did just like he was doing—lit out looking for times to get better or so a woman he left couldn't find him. If something terrible was to happen to one of you children, I could get hold of your daddy through the railroad. But a whole lot can happen to a chile on the way to terrible. Look at Johnnie. When he left outta here, the spirit wasn't in the boy to be a singer, it was *leaving* him. That's *why* he left. He was another man running from a woman, running from all o' us, running from me. Just like his daddy.

"Hassalia, you be the Mama for a little bit and *listen*. I been having dreams scare me bad. I started grieving before Ma Rhetta was gone. Found that out soon as she died, when the breath just went outta her up there in that bed. Like she let go. I was the one letting go of her for the longest time. Damn, I wish I coulda figured that ol' woman out before she left 'way from here. She got away before I was *through* with her.

"She was tight, Hassalia. I know you don't wanna hear me say it right out like that, but that's the Lord's truth. She couldn't give me and Jim and Fanny and Gregory but so much time. She kept everything close, didn't talk too much about her menfolks. Didn't wanna or didn't know how, I don't know which. She was tight, close in, hard. Maybe if she hadna been she never coulda made it.

"Me and her were more alike than you'da thought. She was kinda small, and me, I'm kinda big. But it was a funny business, me and her carrying like we were at the same time, me with Johnnie and her with Gregory. Lord, didn't folks talk about that. We let 'em talk.

"But since she died I'm dreaming like a crazy woman. I'm almost howling myself awake from some of this dreaming.

"Dreamed more than once. And it's always the same. In this dream, I'm sitting in a chair upstairs, in my bedroom.

And I'm wide open. I got my clothes on, but I'm cut open from my neck right down between my breasts all the way down to my stomach. I'm gashed open. But it don't hurt a little bit. And you can look inside me and see all my insides just a working away, digesting food and all o' that, just as clear, like you were watching TV.

"Next thing I know, Ma Rhetta comes in. Only she's real young, she's a pretty young girl, with an old-timey kinda dress on. It's kinda tight on her and she looks like she can get a man if she wanna, real easy. She's all saucy acting and real cute, and she's even got a parasol to go with her red dress. I know it's her, even if she is real young. But she doesn't know who I am right off. I say, 'Mama, you looking so young and pretty. Where you going?' I'm just real glad to see her looking fine like she does. I don't even think about me being all open like I am. I know she's seeing my insides showing clear as can be, but I'm hoping she won't say anything.

"She says, 'You know, I'm gon' have to find somebody to take me to the fair, lookin' pretty like I do. I got to find the right man or this dress'll go for nothing, nothing at all.' I say, 'Well, good as you look, finding a man to take you to the fair won't be hard.' Then, like she knows me all of a sudden, she says, 'Oh, but, Ruby, it's harder than you *think*, girl.' She's talking real saucy and friendly, like the two of us were girls the same age together, with nothing to think about but good looking young men.

"She says, 'Honey, it's not gon' be easy. See, the fair's way yonder 'cross the hollow, and my daddy don't 'llow me to go over there with no man no kinda way. He done told me too many times, any man taking a gal 'cross that hollow can't have no good notion about the quality of that gal's bringing up. And I don't want my daddy nor nobody else to be thinking bad of me. So I got to get me a man who can take me 'cross the hollow to the colored folks' fair and bring me back home safe—before nightfall. My daddy don't stand for no trifling too late into the evening. I got to get a quality man, quality. What mus' I do, Ruby?'

"I say, 'Well, Mama, I don't rightly know. I've been looking for quality myself many a day, and I haven't found it once.' I'm sitting there still wondering if she sees my insides all open.

"Then my stomach commences to making noise like insides do, digesting food. It gets loud. She still doesn't say anything. She's just twirling around in her pretty dress not thinking about anything but how she's gon' get some man to take her to the colored fair.

"Finally the noise gets so bad I've *got* to say something. So I say, feeling real 'shamed about all o' this noise, 'Mama, I don't know how I come to be open like I am, with my insides making all o' this noise. I sure didn't mean for you to have to bother with it.' She kinda sniffs up in the air and says, 'Ruby, I'm trying to find me somebody to take me to the colored fair, and you making noise on your insides so no man's gonna wanna come around here. You're spiting me with all o' that noise.

"I say, 'No, truthfully, Mama, I didn't know this was gon'happen. I'd be right pleased if you go to the fair.' But then she turns on me. She doesn't wanna hear anything I've got to say. 'Hmpf!' she says, and throws her head up in the air.

"I say, 'Mama, you see how I'm open like I am? I was just sitting here and this happened. I musta brought it down on me some way. It's like I'm a house, Mama, and my skin is a big window. I can see out, and folks can see in, too. I don't feel like somebody anymore, Mama. I feel like I'm a house.'

"She says, 'Gal, you just talkin' like this 'cause you want *my* house. You know you ain't s'posed to take it—but go on and take it. Just take it. I'm lookin' for a man to carry me to the colored fair. I ain't studyin' no house. Go on and take

136

the house, Ruby. *Take* it.' She's real disgusted with me now. And I say, 'Mama, it's not this house I'm thinking about.'

"She goes to turning around the room in her pretty red dress and spinning her red parasol. That parasol gets going faster and faster, and it starts throwing things in the room around and around. It doesn't pick up me sitting in the chair. But it takes all the furniture and everything in the room, 'til finally the walls fall down and I'm sitting up on the second floor with nothin' around me or the house.

"Mama hangs on to her red parasol and floats up in the air. And she laughs. She says, 'Ruby, I tol' you to go on and take the house, girl. I ain't studyin' this house. And now, look, it's blowin' away.

"'I'm goin' to the colored fair on my own, girl. I'll find a man when I get there. Your ol' loud, smelly insides ain't gon' stop no man from findin' me. And look, Ruby, look, you ain't got no house now.' She's laughing and spinning around in the sky, just aholding on to her red parasol and looking pretty and fine as she can be, floating on to that fair and leaving me there with the wind and the dust blowing all around. I wave to her. I say, 'Bye, Mama. I'm glad my insides making noise like they did didn't keep a man from you. Have a good time at the colored fair. I'll be all right.' She's laughing and she floats over the hill and 'cross the hollow.

"I know she's happy. I haven't got a house. But I'm not worrying any more, not when I see her floating 'cross the sky like she is. Seems to me like I'm gon' get back a house some kinda way. And my insides stop making noise and close right up, like somebody turned off their TV. I'm sitting there all out in the open up on the second floor, with no walls around me. But I don't hurt any more."

*

Jim. "Don't be cuttin' your eyes at me, Hassalia."

*

Esther. "Hassalia, bring Beetsy up here to my room. I don't feel like going downstairs. Mama wanna see her baby girl."

*

Sting Ray. "What do I look like to you, Hassalia, some kinda fool? You think I'm gon' stay poor just 'cause Esther used to it? No, girl, that ain't what I'm meanin' to do, stay poor."

*

Gregory. "Hassalia, Mama woulda left it all to Ruby anyway. You know Fanny's not looking for anything. Me and Lyelle either. Jim? You know well as I do, Jim's always gon' look out for Jim. He wasn't counting on Mama 'live or dead to help him. Not that nigger.

"You think maybe you got a rich uncle, Hassalia? A whole lot of folks in Crawley think so. And they're sure not talking about me. Ask your rich Uncle Jim how rich he is. You'll find out, Jim couldn't be waiting on nothing of Mama's, 'cause he don't need nothing of hers. He lived off of her for how many years? Lived in her house like he didn't have to go nowhere. I guess he didn't. He sure stayed. And I'll bet you he got some money to show for it.

"And look at who left, Hassalia. Johnnie and Izell. They got out. And me, when me and Lyelle got married. So, what are you gonna do? You been staying there alla this time thinking about Mama and Ruby and Esther and Beetsy, and even M'Lady. And now, with Mama gone, it doesn't make sense to you, does it? Did it ever? Not to Fanny, either, that's for sure. She got hell from that house. And she can't even say she got out. She was put out, Hassalia. You gonna let 'em put you out, too?"

*

Ruby. "Find a way to keep quiet, Hassalia. You're making more noise than I can stand right now, knocking and banging around this house. You gon' fall down and hurt yourself you don't stop."

*

Fantelle. "I wouldna said I was a bad person. But maybe I was. Maybe I brought more hurt into this world than was in the world before I got here. I watch Son-Son—can't call him "little", but he is only a chile—and I see such brightness and life in that boy's eyes. He's so big and pretty and anxious about every little thing growing out in his Mama's garden or whatever thing he can get into that his daddy's working on around the house. He's so alive. I partake of this chile's happiness but I couldn't tell you what his happiness is made of. I only know it's a happiness I never had. I don't begrudge the chile, nor hold it against him.

"But where is mine? Did I let it get away from me when I was a girl? Nobody had to tell me I wasn't pretty. Why did people look at me like I didn't know? I wasn't aching to be pretty. I was aiming to be somebody folks would pay some mind to. I ushered at the church, was Sunday school secretary, was helpmeet to the sick like Reverend Jonas said we all should be, made some of the best potato salad anybody ever did for the church picnic every summer from when I was fourteen. Worked hard to make it so folks would like it. But the next day folks would forget I was the same person, still needing praise.

"Mama didn't praise. Mama noticed me if I did something she didn't like. But if I just did like I was s'posed to, she wouldn't say anything to me. Funny how I was the one folks would ask on the street how we were doing at our house. I was the one. I was a carrier of the message of my Mama's house out to the world. You wouldna thought it, but I was. It got so folks expected me to know how Mama felt and what she was doing and what Ruby and Jim were doing and what they were thinking about and planning on—like they figured I couldn't have plans of my own. I wasn't pretty enough, or smart like I coulda gone to the city and made my way like some colored women do. And the white girls sure weren't my friends.

"Had a friend once, name of Alberta. I was ten the first time I laid eyes on her. She was the world to me. For a little while. When her folks came through here, there were a whole lot of 'em—ten children. And all of 'em used to work together in the fields. Picking. Most of the time down south. When they came through here they were working way out on the highway, picking apples. Short season, they said. They were here two weeks that first year, and two weeks the year after that. The first year, Alberta and I just played together—jacks and jump rope and you-show-me-yours, like little girls will do. I had some dolls and things, they weren't hardly anything, but she was so glad to have 'em to play with. I even gave her one. She was just as gentle with those dolls. She would talk to 'em so nice; she could go on and on making up stories about having those dolls with her on the road. I would sit and listen to her. She and her folks were poor something pitiful, but she acted like some day they were gonna have a house and she could go to school at the same school all the time, instead of traveling around like they did. This ol' house of ours was like magic to her. Mama didn't mind her being around so much 'cause she was so quiet and respectful.

"When she came back the next year, she was older. I didn't understand how much older than me she was. She had a baby in the time she was gone. It died out there in the cold in one of those shacks where they let people stay who

140

pick all the time. She had the baby in the shack. Her Mama and some other women were there. She said it was a pretty little boy. But it looked to her like they couldn't feed it right, she said, 'cause the baby kept on fretting even when she gave it her breast. Got weaker and weaker and just died.

"When she told me this her voice didn't have any crying in it. She said it straight out, like it wasn't even her who had the baby and watched it die, like it happened to somebody else. She just stopped by to see me, she said, to tell me how much fun we had the year before when she passed through this way. She didn't want to play with dolls this time, said she didn't even want to see 'em, thanks just the same.

"I asked her who was the baby's daddy. She said it was some tall skinny boy who picked with 'em, she didn't know him from anybody else and only saw him that one time. I said, 'You gonna have another baby, Alberta, and get married and live in a house, like you said?' She said, 'Don't know where the daddy's coming from, but if another one did come along, I sure don't feel like no mama inside no more. Why did my baby have to die like that?' I told her I didn't know. She left after that, and I've never seen her back in Crawley since.

"But she was my friend, Hassalia. And she lost something that was hers, that she tried to hold on to. The same with me, only it wasn't a baby. Come to that, I was my own baby. It was just me trying to come into myself and get some respect without a man. That's what was mine, what I was trying to hold on to. What I gave birth to. And it crawled and cried and puked and dirtied itself and walked and taught itself how to talk. I raised it. So it talks back to me now. What I lost, that's my baby. Respect. I can feel it inside. Nobody else can see it, touch it, claim it. But it's mine. And now it's tall and strong, Hassalia. It's what keeps my spine straight even when my mind goes away from me.

"And I feel kinda like Alberta. She did what she was

s'posed to do, all she knew how to do. She had the baby. It died. Mine, what I'm calling my baby, lived. But we were both looking for respect. Still looking. Not foolish enough to wait forever for it. But still looking."

∗

Jim. "You ain't seen your Mama upset like this before, Hassalia. I have. Don't worry her, lookin' at her all the time like you do. Leave the woman be. She ain't like you. She don't have no Mama no more. Didn't know what to do with her when she had her, now don't know what to do without her. I know. But she don't. Let her alone, Hassalia. You ain't gonna have *her* one of these days. Then we'll see what you do."

∗

Sting Ray. "You think I'm not gon' take Esther 'way from here, you wrong. You gon' have to make it the best way you can, girl. I know she your sister, but she don't need to be layin' up in no house feeling bad all the time. Your Mama ain't fit right now, Hassalia. I don't know what all is goin' on around here, but all of y'all best believe I ain't standin' for no foolishness. It come time for me to take Esther and my baby girl 'way from here, that's what I'm gon' do. Pack up and be gone. Don't be lookin' at me like you got some kinda claim on me and her, Hassalia. You ain't the boss of us."

∗

Esther. "Stop *botherin'* me, Hassalia. You look at me like I'm crazy. I ain't crazy, honey. What I am is smart, you hear me? Smart. Sting Ray gon' get me and Beetsy 'way from

142

here. What you want me to say about Ma Rhetta? She's gone. She left this world before she wanted to, is all I know. But it wasn't up to me, Hassalia. You act like somebody took Ma Rhetta 'way from you particular. She wasn't your property, Hassalia."

*

Ruby. "Hassalia, bring me a blanket. I just wanna lay here for a while. Don't say anything to anybody. Jim come in from off the truck, don't say anything, you hear me?"

*

Sting Ray. "I got bid'ness and I'm leaving outta here now, Hassalia. I'll be back in a few days. I ain't sayin' just when. Esther still actin' so goddamn simple when I get back I'm gon' find out the reason why. And you niggers best come up with some kinda answer. Bet' not play with me, none of y'all."

*

Jim. "You don't know what I'm thinking, Hassalia. You wanna call yourself knowing. But you don't know. Ma Rhetta's the first somebody taken away from you and you don't know how to act behind it. Your Daddy was taken from you, too, but you don't wanna say that. Your Daddy left is what you've been sayin', what your Mama started you sayin', so you don't know what else to say. But he was taken. You think women kept him out on the road all o' these years. Making money. Living fast. You think he's havin' himself a good time out there, don't you? Do you know what it's like, Hassalia, to carry a tray of glasses filled with champagne from one end of a railroad car to the other, bobbin' and weavin' so that little white lady comin' down the aisle doesn't fall and hurt herself, so you can get ready to serve her and her husband and their friends and the folks they just met up with that champagne, 'cause they're celebratin' some *more* money they got hold of just before they got on that train? Do you know what it's like to try to *sparkle* like one of those glasses when you serve them, Hassalia, 'cause those folks think the glasses and the champagne and you are there for them—not for you, for them?

"A Negro like your daddy workin' on those trains has got to sparkle, Hassalia. Shine. You know what it takes to smile that much, dazzle those folks' eyes for two thousand miles so they think they're not just on a train but near 'bout on the way to heaven they're so comfortable, so happy? You're takin' care of those folks with your smile, your dazzlin' walk, your hands just as fast and strong and steady.

"If you're your Daddy, you've been taken, Hassalia. You can say you don't belong to those folks, but who do you belong to? You belong to that railroad? No, you don't own that railroad. You're a Pullman porter, and Randolph and his folks had to fight to get you respect like a union person. And I mean *fight*. The railroad folks didn't want to give Randolph and the Pullman porters any kinda recognition. 'Keep servin', keep smilin', you belong to us.'

"Do you belong to your family? If Izell shows up here he's gon' have your Mama down on him so hard all he can do is turn around and walk back out the door. He doesn't belong here 'cause he doesn't own anything, Hassalia. He's already been taken. He belongs to those folks he's workin' for. Why do you think he's not here with you, bad as you want him to be? Because on the road he can rub two quarters together. If he stays here, he can dig a ditch and stay in one if he wanna, the folks won't care. 'Cause they aren't gon' let him own the ditch, Hassalia. He'll only get so much before somebody—somebody white—says, Stop. I don't care how far he goes, they're gon' say, Stop. Because we don't own our own self, Hassalia. Never did. If a black man wanna own his own self, he's in the wrong country. You tell the white man that Negroes helped make this country, he'll sa,: 'What have niggers ever made but jazz, babies and trouble?'

"All right, you'll say to me, 'Jim, look at you. You're doin' for yourself. You're in business. You own a car and a couple of trucks, you're drivin' one of the trucks and you hire somebody time by time to drive the other one. You're the one runnin' your business. Nobody tells you what to do. You own the thing.'

"You're right. But s'pose I want to be the biggest and the best of what I do? I don't just wanna own a car and a couple of trucks and a yard full of junk. Play like I wanna own a whole *lot* of junk, Hassalia. All the junk there is in this town and in all the towns around here. I want to own that junk. Who would care? Why? What is it, but junk? Who cares if one Negro man—me—owns it all?

"But there are folks in Crawley and hereabouts, in these other little towns, who won't let me do that, Hassalia. They'll only let a black man own so much of anything, includin' junk.

"See, Hassalia, there are regular folks and there are Rockefellers in everything, all down the line. There's a Rockefeller of cement and a Rockefeller of grocery stores and a Rockefeller of garbage haulin' and a Rockefeller of whorehouses and a Rockefeller of this coffee you see me drinkin'.

"And let's just say all I wanna be in this town is the Rockefeller of junk, Hassalia. Junk. These folks aren't gonna let me. No, they aren't. The white man tradin' junk in the next town is watchin' me. Especially if the folks there—black or white, it doesn't make any difference—want

145

to deal with me. That man doesn't want me there too much or too long, 'cause if I get to dealin' with too many of those folks and they get to like doin' business with me, I may wanna start ownin' somethin' in that town, Hassalia.

"Not just dealin' junk in that town but ownin' some of that junk, a whole lot of it, for a long time—and the land it's sittin' on. Unh-unh. Can't have that. Why not? 'Cause if I get to ownin' too much I'm on the way to becomin' the Rockefeller of that, Hassalia, I mean as far as these little bit of towns around here go. Now, I know what you're thinkin': none of the white people are the Rockefeller of junk, either. I'm not sayin' they are. But they've got a whole lot of other things they can do if junk doesn't do right by them. Or maybe there isn't a whole lot they can do, some of 'em. They're the ones who all the more don't want me to be the Rockefeller of junk, just 'cause they can't be. They aren't gon' let anybody colored be the Rockefeller of anything. Any time. Anywhere.

"So what are we Negroes the Rockefellers of, Hassalia? I'll tell you what. We're the Rockefellers of misery. Misery back. Years, generations, centuries. We gots a plenty, thank you. And they don't want that. They don't even want to see it. That's why they pay your Daddy to smile at 'em while he's carryin' that tray, and why they want him to keep on steppin' and not drop it. 'Cause as long as he's doin' that he doesn't own anything, isn't actin' like he wants to own anything, isn't turnin' into the Rockefeller of anything."

*

Gregory. "Too much remembering, Hassalia. I know. I think about Ma Rhetta constant now. All day.

"What do you think she meant when she told me I shouldn't pay any mind to outdoing Johnnie?

"Johnnie couldna been a friend to me. I didn't know how

to be a friend to my own self. Lyelle's the only friend I ever had, truthful. I got married to her on a humble. I didn't have the nerve for doing it, so that's why I did it. Folks could laugh. But I did it. Johnnie wasn't the one who hurt me. Why did Mama keep telling me not to worry so bad about him? All y'all thought I was worrying my mind about Johnnie. I wasn't worried about that boy. I was wondering what was happening to that boy, like we all were.

"I wonder where he could be, Hassalia. He doesn't write. Jim oughta be able to find out something about what happened to Johnnie and where he is now. He knows enough of those bad ol' niggers in the city. He could find out if somebody did Johnnie in. He could still find out, even if it happened a long time ago.

"It's so sad to let anybody go like that. They go away and you can't hear from 'em. I know you think about Izell, Little Man. But Izell always had far away in his eyes. All you had to do was look in 'em. I know you didn't see that in his eyes. You saw him looking at you and all you could think about was making him stay here with you. But Izell was kinder to you than you thought, Has. Truthful, he was. It's hard on you, but when he went away he was doing the rightest thing he knew to do.

"But Johnnie, he wasn't made for going away, like Izell was. Johnnie was so sad going away. He talked like he was happy, but if you could listen under his singing he was sad down there where his voice came from. It was sadness, not music, that was coming outta him. He missed Izell worse than you do. He just couldn't say it out loud. He's a man. Not s'posed to be missing his daddy who left him. S'posed to be mad. But Johnnie wasn't mad, he was sad. That's why he would strut so. I know, 'cause I couldn't strut like he did. If I didn't stay right here and get married to Lyelle I'da been sadder than him."

*

M'Lady. "I only want to sit here by the window, for now. I
will go on caring for myself. You have all been more than
kind. I have spent time among colored people and always
found them warm and decent. This house has been like that.
Ever since your grandmother found me and told your
mother to bring me here. Me, an old woman with no place
to go. I could only say thank you inside, to myself. I couldn't
see you or hear you except as if I was under water. I've felt
the people in this house every minute I was here. But I could
say nothing. I can say little now. I'm tired.

"You, young child, are blessed and cursed at the same
time, like me. Here but not here. My mind was away. Now
it is coming back. I've been on a long journey. I've never
been to Africa. But I am so tired now, in this house, that it
feels as though I have been there and back. Me, an old white
woman who, yes, has lived among the colored in her time
but would not say she could read their hearts. But here I am.
And being here among you, locked in silence, has been like
a stop on a long journey. Sitting in a chair, not able to speak,
able to see and hear dimly. Feeding myself and caring for
myself and being privileged enough to be able to clean
myself, and feel a fresh nightgown on my body and not
being able to thank the person who let me have it. I want
to thank you now. But not all of you are here any longer, I
know. I know your grandmother is gone. She left you—you
in particular, young woman—sooner than you wanted or
could see any need for.

"But are you sure she is gone? Her mind may be
searching around outside this house right now trying to find
a way back into it. She, too, may only be on a journey, as I've
been. When you tell me your name and her name and your
mother's and your sister's, to me they sound full of journeys
and places: Rhetta, Ruby, Esther, Hassalia, and the child,

Clara, the one you call Beetsy. These don't sound to me like the names of people who are standing still. Your grandmother could be moving deeper into her name, occupying it, taking it up, taking it where it hasn't been before. Names are older than we are, they've been here longer. They outlast us. Think. 'Rhetta'. Where does a name like that end?

"How do you know your grandmother is any further away from you now than I was, sitting right in this chair but unable to speak to any of you? I wonder, because I am not all the way back from where I was. My mind went on a long, long journey and couldn't take my body. It must have been that my body needed to rest and wait for my mind to return. That's why it crippled me in the legs and put me in a wheelchair. To rest. To wait. Here.

"And you, Hassalia, will see that your grandmother needed to rest, too. She is somewhere now, waiting. Maybe waiting for word from this house. You can't say that she isn't, because look at what this house—a house where I was a stranger, after all—did for me. It took me in and allowed me to wait here. Your mother did not know me. Nor did your grandmother. I come from a life that began far from here, that much I can remember now. I will remember more. All that I can remember I will put in your hands, Hassalia.

"You see how well I said that again, your name? Hassalia. What a mysterious name. It summons anyone who hears it and curls itself around them. It's a powerful name. And I just said it for the first time a few minutes ago. Said it because already I've begun to remember it.

"Do you see, Hassalia, how all knowing is, right away, remembering? To know anything is to get it from the past. So, how can we say how far back into the past we must go in order to learn? Except for what strikes us in the face without warning, everything we know we get, right away, from the past, so once you start going back there is no reason to stop at any one time or place, at any one name. Learning could take us far, far back.

"And we know now that there was a time when I was not to remember, not to move, but to give my soul release and time to travel. To go forward, I mean, which is where your grandmother, Rhetta, may be now. Just forward of us, waiting for us. I, we now see, was just backward of you, waiting. Fallen silent, while my soul journeyed. For this journey, this duty, this obligation, this penance my soul was asked to endure, I could have simply been cast in the streets, or allowed to reach a river or an ocean and to drown there. Yet I came into this house to be readied for the next part of the journey.

"And while I was here and my body rested, waited, my soul was wandering, Hassalia, across the world. My soul is not rested. It is only now coming into the quiet to rest. It needs me ready to receive it. That must be why I'm now able to speak again. To you. To remember. And I will remember, I'm sure, all that I have to remember.

"It must seem like some grotesque accident, some demon working its sly magic, to have me, a white woman, here in your house and needing you all so, for so long. And why should you, who have little, share it with a stranger who could see her need for food and shelter and so, take them, but not even give a proper thanks for all she was being given? The thanks had to wait, too. You see, there was some duty your mother and grandmother were performing, something they were answering, when they took me in. Did they know? You and I will ask your mother. We can't any longer ask your grandmother. But her going was part of my soul's returning. I feel that. I can't replace her for you, even though I feel you want her, or someone like her, back. I'm not here to bring her back to you, or to stand in for her in your hearts. But since I was here in this house before she fell ill, I saw and felt, even if I couldn't say it, her leavetaking, her going outward.

"I felt it, Hassalia, the struggle and the letting go. And now it's as if a new struggle will begin. My wandering soul is coming back to do what it must, here. My body has rested. It is not a strong body, yet. And I will never be young again. But my body will get stronger. Where has my soul been? Somewhere dark and hot, Hassalia, wet and full of growing things. That is all I know now. All I can say. Thanks, to be sure. But I will be saying that to you for the rest of my days, wherever the rest of my days take me. And you, lovely Hassalia, blessed and cursed, will know why my thanks are as real as my going on."

*

Jim. "You walk around here lookin' like somebody owes you somethin', Hassalia. You lose something? Something you can't find you useta could? Nobody's s'posed to do for you what you can't do for yourself, Hassalia. Nobody no time is gon' make it easy for you to be colored in this world. If you've got a bad ol' Uncle Jim it gets even harder, doesn't it?

"You saw me with your Mama? You saw me with Esther? You think you're smart? You think maybe you're next? Well, you're not, girl, 'cause you don't know nothin' about nothin'. I'm the one who knows how it all goes, Hassalia, all of it. And you can look out of your face at me all you wanna. That isn't gon' make the world different or me different or your Mama or Esther different.

"Sit down, Hassalia, when I'm talkin' to you. Don't be actin' funny with me. Sit down, I said. You can go when I get through.

"You know your Mama isn't feelin' right or actin' right. She's still shook up behind Ma Rhetta passin' like she did, early. Nobody believed she was gon' go that soon.

151

Hardworkin' woman, but it didn't look like she was gonna give out like she did. That's hard on your Mama.

"And you're not helpin' your Mama none, actin' out like you doin'. What you saw me and your Mama doin' ain't nobody's business, not even yours. You ain't the first one in the world to see it. And me and your Mama ain't the first ones to do it, either.

"There she is now, callin' for you. Go up there and talk to her. And don't act like you're the judge sittin' in the courthouse, you understand me?"

∗

Ruby. "Get me a blanket, Hassalia, please, out of the bottom of the chifforobe there. I'm cold. Tremblin'. Just need to rest here a little bit. I'm not at myself, Lord knows. Don't know why I'm so *cold.*

"Sit here for a minute. Don't go. I know you never saw your Mama like this. I've never been like this. Don't know what's happenin'.

"You always were a taking chile. I was taken with you from when you were born. I know you never did think I thought that, but I did. From when you were little you were skinny and dark and pretty, movin' round this house like a princess from over in Africa. Tall. Like you knew where you we re goin'. That's why we called you Little Man from that day when you put on your Daddy's hat. And you kept on goin'. The rest of us didn't know where you were goin'. I guess we still don't know. Waitin' on you to tell us.

"Don't look away like that when I'm talkin' to you, Hassalia. Don't do that. What kinda Mama are you gon' be one day, if you turn away from your Mama like you're doin' now?

"You think Ma Rhetta was a saint, but she wasn't, Hassalia. Don't open your mouth tryin' to say you don't.

152

You do. She told you about herself and what she been through, I know. Much as she could tell you. And that was somethin'. Wasn't easy for her to do that.

"But you still haven't changed your way of seein' this thing. She's still perfect to you, even if she did wrong sometimes. You've got room in your heart for her, 'cause she's your grandmama and not your mama. She's not the one who has to say no to you. She's not the one fussin' at you. I'm the one doin' that. And you don't think I'm anywhere near 'bout a saint. Unh-unh. Not your bad ol' Mama.

"But you shoulda seen Ma Rhetta when we were comin' up, Hassalia. Me and Jim. Then me and Jim and Fanny. Then Gregory. She wasn't easy, chile. She fed us all right. But her mind wasn't really with her children 'til she had her last one. Stopped havin' 'em, I mean. When she had Gregory. Tryin' to put herself at her ease about menfolks, what menfolks wanted, and why none of hers stayed around.

"I don't know if she ever got it straight in her mind. All I know now is, she's gone and I don't know what to do any more. I can't get at myself. Can't get myself outta this bed.

"I keep thinkin' she's gon' come shufflin' around one of these corners in her bathrobe. Do you? I can feel her. She's not really gone, seems like. But she is.

"So, I took to my bed. Folks'll be talkin' soon, if I don't get up from here. But I can't think about folks, I can't think about goin' to church, I can't think about prayin', I don't want Reverend Jonas anywhere around here. I'm not fit.

"That's what you're thinkin' now, I know. You saw your Mama doin' somethin' awful with your uncle and you don't know how to act. Don't you look away from me. Don't hold your head down. Lift your head up, Hassalia, and look at me when I'm talkin' to you. I'm the only Mama you're ever gon' have. Don't sit there thinkin' somethin' or somebody—

your Daddy, maybe—is gon' come up out of the floor and carry you off somewhere away from me.

"No, Hassalia, that wasn't the first time me and Jim did what we did. Look at me, girl. No, that wasn't the first time. The first time was when I wasn't but fifteen and he was thirteen. Taller than me, but still just a boy. And me a girl. And we were clingin' to each other, Hassalia. Your grandmama didn't have her mind on us. Her mind was still someplace else.

"Wasn't too long after that I met up with your Daddy. Foolish and handsome he looked to me, with a gap-toothed smile you couldn't help but smile back at. He was a slick ol' thing. All of 20 years old. He looked real old to me. Like he was a man. And he was, kinda. He was from outta town and moved slow but steady, like these Southern black boys know how to do from walkin' barefoot on those dirt roads. Those niggers *feel* the earth under their feet. That's why they can look so pretty when they walk. Know all about not hardly wearin' shoes except Sunday—'til they get up size enough to buy their own. Folks wonder why the Negro man loves a pair of shoes. They forget that's when he first could figure he was some kinda grown—when he could buy himself some shoes besides the boots he had to wear in a cotton gin or haulin' wood out in some lumber camp or workin' on a chain gang if he ran completely outta luck. When he could buy some pretty shoes for Sunday. And Sat'dy night. And he had to shine 'em both days. That's when he knew he was grown.

"Anyway, here come your Daddy. And I was this simple little 16-year-old girl. More country than him, even if I was born up north. Your Daddy didn't pay any of that any attention. He thought us northern Negroes were just foolin' ourselves if we thought the white man wanted us. Your Daddy was glad to get north 'cause it got him—finally—to workin' on the railroad. But he didn't come up here thinking it was the colored man's heaven. He had more sense than that.

"What did I know but after a little while I was carryin'? And when Mama found out about it she just said, 'Well, girl, I didn't mean for you to get like I did, young as you are. But at least this one's decent and wants to marry you. Comes from people, Southern people. They too po' to come up here after him, but if he can he'll bring 'em on up here and you'll have you somemore somebodies besides yo' tired Mama to look to. So go on and marry him, girl, and raise the baby on up. This man's got spirit, I'll say that for him. And he ain't scared of workin'. You don't see that all the time in the Negro. Don't study what folks say. They'll talk about you, you marry him or you don't marry him. Go on and do what you got to do.'

"So, me and your Daddy got married. And here come Esther. I had this little baby. First off I was gon' stay home with her. He did cleanin' and haulin' and road work and every other kinda thing. Workin' man, your Daddy, I'll never say he wasn't. But he couldn't make nothing much here. Couldn't get too much ahead. We got us a little ol' place back of Healeys'. It wasn't much more than one room. But it was ours and we were married.

"We would come down here to see Mama and Jim and Fanny. Fanny wasn't but a little thing. Jim was getting where he would poke his mouth out about everything, mad at nobody knew what. Even then he was startin' to work with ol' man Lacey collectin' junk. You don't remember ol' Lacey. He's gone now. He had a little cart he would walk around with. It had two big wheels and a big, loud bell. He would ring that bell and tell you he'd pay what he could for what you didn't want. He'd give you two pennies for a rusty ol' pot, a nickel for a wash tub, a quarter for a pig iron kettle you did everything from boil laundry to smoke ham in. He would carry it out on the highway, piled up in his cart, to the county junk yard, and the white folks would pay him a little somethin' for it. Jim got to seein' how the folks weren't payin' him what he could get if he worked on some of that junk and didn't just turn it over to the folks to melt it down. Jim showed him how he could sell from folks, colored or white, to other folks, instead of just givin' it over to the county. The county called it removal. He was just pickin' up trash so *they* didn't have to pick it up. Jim showed ol' Lacey they were treatin' *him* like trash.

"Anyhow, your Daddy and me, we'd come down here and visit pretty regular. Jim gettin' grown, startin' to see lady folks. Me and Mama used to tease him about bein' a man. And I just knew I was grown, too. Married with this little baby girl coming up. Seemed like everything was on the way to—somewhere. I didn't know where. I sure didn't.

"Your Daddy was the one who told me. I do thank him for that. I didn't then. But I do now. That was what made it some kinda decent. But I went out o' my head when it happened. I couldn't see it no kinda way. Couldn't understand it. Didn't for a long time. It was what your Ma Rhetta couldn't tell you, Hassalia. What she wanted to tell you, just so you'd have the truth in your hands. But she couldn't do it. She left it to me. Like she left a lot to me all along. I've been seein' after Jim since I was four. Still not through. And I'm still lookin' after what Ma Rhetta started but couldn't finish. What she started to tell you but couldn't finish.

"I came up carryin' again. Johnnie. And the very same time, Mama came up carryin', too. We used to have our time of the month together when I was a girl. We were that close. She was that fresh a woman. Still young lookin'. We stopped comin' due at the same time after I moved back of Healeys' with my husband and little baby girl. So, when we came up carryin' the same time, the first thing we did was laugh. It was like our time of the month together again. I didn't ask her right then who the daddy was. I didn't wanna know. That was her.

"So, we were both gettin' bigger. Me carryin' Johnnie and her carryin' Gregory. And folks talked, Lord how they talked. I didn't pay any attention. I didn't know who the man was. Mama wasn't courtin'. But I wasn't livin' here any more, not then. So I didn't know who mighta come callin', or what time of the night. That was what folks were sayin', of course. 'Somebody did some creepin',' was the way niggers put it. Laughin'. But who?

"Do you know who it was, Hassalia? Gregory's daddy? It was your Daddy, Hassalia. It was Izell. He was the one comin' down here on the sly and bein' with Ma Rhetta. And I didn't even know it. My husband and my mama.

"Don't walk away from here. Sit back down in that chair. And don't look like that. It's not easy to say it. It wasn't easy bein' there when it happened. I listened. You can listen. You're a grown woman, Hassalia. Listen.

"Izell was the one who told me. He was mad when he did it. I don't think he wanted to. He probably wouldna if he wasn't mad. But we got to fussin' one night over somethin', I don't even remember what. I was big as a house carryin' Johnnie. And Ma Rhetta was about due, too. And we were fightin', not evil, I didn't think, just fussin'.

"And he turned to me in the middle of it all and said, 'Woman, don't run me outta here with your mouth. I'll be gone tomorrow if you keep actin' like you're doin', and a whole lotta folks'll be glad to see me gone, come and tell you, "You're a lucky woman to be rid of that no good man."

"'You don't know what kinda man I am girl. I'm not a respecter of anything or anybody. You and your Mama think you are. But you aren't. So don't act high with me. Your Mama does like a man who tells her what to do, Ruby. I know. She did it for me, you fool, me. I'm the daddy of that baby she's carryin', you can believe it or not. Go ask her. That's *your* Mama. She was that way before I knew anything about her. Are you better than she is? See if you can get her to come back here and tell me you're better than she is.

"'And you go ask her who's the daddy of that baby. You'll see what your Mama can say no to. And what she can say yes to. And maybe you'll stop runnin' me down 'cause I can't get white folks to stop bein' white and let a colored man walk like a man. They're not about to do it. And your Mama's not about to let a colored man get to feelin' too bad about it. I would go down there to help her out. Fix things around the house. You saw me. You didn't see what she was doin'. Wake up, girl. Your Mama's not your Mama. She's a woman grown. I'm a man grown. Go ask her.'

"I was carryin' big as a house, like I say. But I swear to you I didn't walk, I ran—don't know how I looked; musta been a funny kinda runnin'—to this house to talk to Mama. I said to her, 'Izell just told me he's the daddy of that baby you're carryin'. That true?' 'Yes.' That's all. 'Yes.' Then she went on upstairs. Didn't say another word. Looked me in the eye, I'll say that for her. She was a strong ol' heifer, Hassalia, don't you ask me to lie. I stood there in the hallway for I don't know how long. Then I sat down in a chair for I don't know how long. The house was dead quiet. I looked up and saw I was in my nightgown. I had left the house without puttin' on a robe or anything. Just came straight down the street. I caught a chill. Then I got myself up and walked home.

"Before long, we both had the babies. Then Izell stopped gettin' regular work around here and went on the road. Sometimes he made money out there and would send some to me. Sometimes he didn't. Hardly wrote. I didn't know from one month to the next how much I was gon' have to eat on. Got to where I had to give up our little ol' place behind Healeys'. All me and Esther and Johnnie could do was come back here and live with Mama. Izell wasn't

workin' on the railroad yet. He was doin' some of everything on the road. And time by time he would come to see
us. I started takin' in laundry. Had to do somethin' to help
Mama. Just the two of us. Folks talkin' about us bad. It
wasn't easy. She was glad for the comp'ny.

"Izell would kinda come back to see both of us. He was
never with Mama anymore that way. Never. I'm sure of
that. Him and me would be together when he was here. He
was happy about you, Hassalia. He was. I could see it on his
face when he looked at you after you were born. He was
happy. But the house and all, Mama and all. The children—
Esther, Johnnie, Gregory, then you—it was more than he
knew what to do about. When he was around the house all
you children would laugh and act a fool with him. He liked
that. But Izell just couldn't stay. Never could. He was that
kinda man from the start. And with Ma Rhetta havin'
Gregory and me havin' Johnnie together like we did—I don't
think he ever got used to it. A man boastful one minute is
'shamed the next, Hassalia. I don't care how they act.
Menfolks feel shame, too. They just don't show it. They run.

"No. I know what you're thinkin'. No. Your Uncle
Grease doesn't know about this. He thinks his daddy is a
friend of Izell's useta come by here with Izell. That's what
Ma Rhetta told him. And the man died. We didn't disturb
his way of thinkin' about it all these years.

"Lord, Hassalia, I'm so *cold.*

"A woman doesn't always know what she's gonna do.
She doesn't know when she's gonna get lonely or who's
gon' be there to ease the hurt. When me and your Daddy
had you, I thought maybe him and me were gonna be like
married folks again. Just like you thought he would come
back for you, I thought he would come back for you. But he
hasn't done that. It doesn't mean he doesn't have feelin's for
you. He just doesn't have feelin's for me. You need to
understand that before you leave this house. And you're

gon' leave this house. You're not gon' be like Ma Rhetta and me and Esther and stay in this country town callin' itself the suburbs, full of white folks who still want colored to clean their house and take care of their babies and vote for 'em. And play Aunt Jemima and cook for 'em. You're not gon' be like that. You're gettin' outta here. Workin' at that garage was one way. I know you were mad when the man let you go, but that man can only do what folks around here let him do. And you're not gon' be like Lyelle, either, married to Gregory. They're the shadows of each other, so neither one o' them knows who's castin' the shadow.

"But no matter where you go or what you do, Hassalia, you gon' have to be a woman, and find a way to deal with colored men.

"I didn't know what my feelin's were doin' to me when Jim and me first went together like we were a man and woman who didn't know each other. I was a girl. We were closer than we shoulda been. But there wasn't anybody else in this town we could go to. Folks talked about Ma Rhetta from the time she came here, a woman with no husband and two little children who didn't have right daddies they could lay claim to. That puts a funny feelin' in folks' minds. I don't know where it comes from. But it's always there.

"Then after I met up with your Daddy, there wasn't anything more between me and your Uncle Jim. Nothin'. Jim liked Izell. And Izell liked him fine. Izell would come and go, Hassalia. Your Daddy just isn't particular about stayin' anywhere too long. I didn't know that when I married him. But he'da found some kinda way to get outta here. Interferin' with Ma Rhetta like he did was just the way your daddy figured out to get away from me. From anybody, woulda been. You see he hasn't ever found anybody on the road he stays with either, not for long. Maybe he's got women in other towns he stays with, but he couldn't be stayin' with any of them long either, or he couldn't keep his job. Good job, too. I see why he doesn't wanna give it up. He's not particular about sendin' too much money back home to me, but he figures I'm gon 'tie him down if he sends money, stay mad if he doesn't send any at all, and maybe not bother him too much if he sends just a little bit. So, that's what he sends. A little bit.

"That's hard on a woman. He doesn't jump one way or the other. And Jim's still here. Still. Here.

"Now, with Mama gone, somethin's come over me. I ache, Hassalia, all the time, all over. My muscles, and down deep in my back, and in through my thighs—all of that hurts. Jim touches me and he finds those aches and they don't ache so bad. They don't go away. But they don't ache so bad.

"First thing he said to me when he saw me with almost all o' my clothes off was, 'Lord, woman, where did you get those scars?' Bruises, scars, cuts, scrapes, old sores that healed over but left marks. That's what my body's like now, Hassalia. It wasn't like that when he saw it when I was a girl. How did it get this way? Livin', Hassalia. Growin' old. Not bein' able to forget. That'll give your body scars.

"And I haven't been woman to anybody for so long I forgot how it feels. I'm so bitter mad at your daddy I don't know how to be a woman. Jim opens me up. For hard and for sure he does. Like he can do with anything he takes a mind to. I haven't spread my legs that wide in I don't know how long, Hassalia. Wouldna known I could anymore if he hadn't made me. I said made me, 'cause he knew I was waitin' in myself to do it. Needed to do it. Forgot how to, without meaning to forget. Lord, Hassalia, sometimes I missed your Daddy so bad.

"Ma Rhetta dies on me. I'm not ready, Hassalia, I'm not ready to let that old woman go. I wasn't *through* with her. Damn. What did you kids used to say, 'You have to eat dirt before you die'? That was it, wasn't it? If one of y'all dropped a cookie on the ground, you'd pick it up and dust it off and say, 'You have to eat dirt before you die'. Then eat it. That's how I'm feelin' now. And that's what I'm doin'. Me and Jim both.

"Let me go back to sleep a little bit, now, Hassalia. I'm feelin' better. Warmer too. Don't worry too much, daughter. See there, I can call you 'daughter', too, just like Ma Rhetta called all of us. You're *my* daughter. You and Esther both. And she's got Beetsy. Someday maybe you'll have a little girl o' your own you'll be callin' 'daughter'. But I'm Ma Rhetta's daughter for real, Hassalia, not you. You don't have to be that. Go on and be your own self, girl."

✳

Esther. "No, I ain't gettin' outta this bed 'til I get good and ready. Sting Ray'll be back soon. When he gets back, that's when I'm getting up from here. I ain't cleanin' no more white folks' kitchen floors, you hear me? I ain't. I'ma wait right here for Sting Ray. And Beetsy can wait right here with me, can't you, sugar? We're all right in this bedroom, Hassalia. If I need you, I'll send Beetsy to come and get you, you hear? We gon' wait right here for daddy, ain't we, sugar?"

✳

Fantelle. "How could he do this? How? You couldna known, Hassalia. Don't be blaming yourself. It's too much for anybody to bear. Hold on to me, chile. Just hold on. Aunt Fanny's here. God knows what we're gonna do. God only knows."

✳

M'Lady. "Keep yourself safe, child. If it helps you to stand

162

here in my room and cry, do it. I know it must seem now like there isn't safety anywhere on this earth. That's true.

"It's bad enough that your grandmother's suffering took the toll on her and everyone around her that it did. But it would be even worse to blame anyone who came after her for carrying on and continuing that suffering. That's not what any of you were doing, Hassalia. No one wanted it to go on and no one wanted it to come to this.

"But I don't have any answers for you. I don't know what it means when a man comes into a house where his wife and daughter live and finds the wife has shared a bed with her uncle, Jim. What causes the husband, you wonder, to pull out a gun and shoot his wife through the heart? To wait until after the uncle has left and to go in and to say something to the woman—what, pray God?—and then shoot her dead?

"But that wasn't what he did first. What makes that same woman's *other* uncle—younger than she—come to the house just when the incident is about to happen? Looking to do what? Coming into the house for what? Hearing what? Surely there was talk—no doubt angry, loud talk—between the husband and wife. How much of that did her uncle, Gregory—the man she thought of as her boy uncle, her sad boy uncle, so much less charming and graceful and blessed with beauty than her absent brother—hear? Did it make him walk slowly, surreptitiously, even respectfully, up the stairs, wanting to hear but not wanting to seem as though he wanted to hear, the argument going on? Imagine, Hassalia, the kinds of accusations this husband, if that is what he is to be called to the woman, this father, if that is what he is to be called to his child, could hurl at the woman who had retreated to her bed since the death of Ma Rhetta, just as her own mother had done.

"Imagine the kinds of rage that husband felt and hurled at his wife, the woman he found betraying him with her uncle, a man who had once employed him, a man he would never suspect of such a thing and therefore a man he had no cause to mistrust. And the truth, to that husband, just come back from a journey of who knows what dangers to find his wife had bedded with that same uncle, must have made it clear to him that in fact it was trusting, ever trusting, his wife's uncle that had led to this outrage. He must have been wondering how and if he could have got his wife and daughter out of that house sooner: Would it have kept him from this rage he felt, kept him from feeling such a murderous rush of scorn for her?

"Imagine still more, Hassalia: what such a man would have felt when another man, smaller and frailer than he, his wife's other uncle, in fact, though younger than she, when *that* uncle, that unprepossessing man, came into the house, heard—overheard—the couple arguing, and climbed the stairs to see what he could do for the woman who was his niece but was in fact more like a sister to him, so close were they in years, so often had they played together as children. And when he heard his niece—this woman who was like a sister to him—pleading for her life, something in him must have not been able to let it rest as a simple quarrel between a husband and wife, something in which he would not normally have interfered, this timid man, married, with a giant of a Son and a wife as slender and timid and hardly-there as he.

"Where and what is manhood, Hassalia? Where does a man learn how to do it, to become it, this thing called a man, to pick up this obligation called 'manhood'? And what makes one man think it is his *manhood* he is defending when he attacks his wife whom he finds out has gone to bed with her uncle?

"Is it the same thing that makes another man, much charier than the first, much more a married man—what makes this second man declare it is *his* manhood's duty to protect his niece when she is under what he takes to be attack, taking what he calls abuse, from her husband? About *their* marriage bed. Standing outside the door of their bedroom, what did he think about the charge he heard the husband hurl at the wife? What did this man think he was going to do about the charge—or the woman enduring it, undergoing it? What, precisely, did he imagine he was putting a stop to? Did he enter the room without knocking, hearing the married people arguing and still feeling that he was right to intervene? Why couldn't he have waited outside? Why did he go into that room? What words could he possibly have heard that would make him think that he could come between a husband and wife at such a moment? Did he know whether he would add to their pain or take some of it away when he entered the room? Or did he simply not want this brutal outsider—which is all he could have thought of the husband—to wreak any more havoc, to hurt his niece, whom he had played with from a child?

"What were the two young husbands to do? Why were they fighting each other at a moment like this? Why weren't they friends against a common enemy? What, truly, was at risk? How did this moment blast them apart, one in protection of his niece, one in anger at his wife, in defense of his outraged male honor? How would the slender, cautious husband imagine he could stop the massive, powerful one? He was not the uncle who had taken her physically. He was the uncle *younger* than she, the one she had regarded all her life as a gangling, awkward boy. Never a man, even though he was married just as she was, a parent just as she was. Here he was bursting through a door to defend her against the fury of her husband. Even then, even with her husband's gun pointed at her, did she think of her boyish uncle's 'defense' of her as a hopeless, empty, silly gesture of a man she thought had not yet reached manhood, despite his married state, despite his fatherhood? Surely she must have thought it was her *older* uncle coming back through that door to 'rescue' her. Or at the very least she must have thought the older man was returning to assume his responsibility, to take her husband's rage on himself, he who had taken his niece to bed—*after* taking her mother to bed.

"*So*, she must have thought, *it has to be him coming through the door now with a power to match my husband's.*

"What can she have felt when she saw the slender man who was also her uncle, but whom she thought of as nothing more than an absurdly overaged boy, married by the merest happenstance, a father by one of life's sheer improbabilities, an inexplicable creator of his giant, overgrown Son? There he stood, demanding her husband let her go. And how did her horror grow when she saw the two men struggle over the gun? Can she have realized then that the gun was meant for her, that her husband had come into her room to kill her?

"And how did it happen that the husband of the woman on the bed killed the other husband? And was the husband carrying out his plan when he then turned the gun on his wife? Was that the rest of the plan, or a new idea that came to him only after three bullets had been pumped into the other husband, his wife's ridiculously younger uncle, little more than an overaged skinny boy now bleeding on the bedroom floor? As he pumped the lead into the woman on the bed, what did he tell himself about his daughter, sitting on the floor in the corner of her mother's room on a paisley child's carpet, who, minutes before, had been revealing to her mother the fabled places she 'flew' over on what she called her Magic Carpet?

"He simply ran out the door after he had emptied the gun, without a word to his daughter, who now sat on her Magic Carpet screaming and holding her hands over her ears, so loud had been the report of his pistol as the sound that carried her mother and her great uncle out of this world jumped into her ears and down through her heart into her bowels, where it lodged, cold and still loud, terrifying her with the odor of lead and smoke that filled the room. Her mother and her great uncle were fast leaving her and her world, bleeding onto the floor, their blood seeping into her Magic Carpet, pulling her down from the sky where she rode."

EPILOGUE

HASSALIA, 1979

This is the urgency: Live!
and have your blooming in the noise of the
whirlwind...

All about are the cold places,
all about are the pushmen and jeopardy, theft—
all about are the stormers and scramblers but
what must our Season be, which starts from Fear?
Live and go out...

Conduct your blooming in the noise and whip of the
whirlwind.

–Gwendolyn Brooks
"The Second Sermon on the Warpland"

STING RAY SHOT ESTHER AND GREGORY to death in early November 1957. Beetsy was six years old and saw the whole thing. I couldn't stay in Crawley after that.

I came here to Eli, and been here ever since. I didn't just pick it off the map. But almost. I knew some friends of Roy's who used to drive a truck out here regular. They'd come through Crawley on their way to Chicago, stop there for some more pickups, and then bring it on home to Eli.

Eli isn't but fifty miles from Crawley, over here in Indiana. And it's nigh about as close to Chicago as Crawley. So, I moved, but where did I go?

These friends of Roy's said they were willing to use a colored girl in the office of this one trucking company. I found a place to stay. And the next day I went to the five and dime and bought a couple of cheap little dresses and some black shoes and went in there to work. I didn't even think twice. I knew I had to come outta those pants.

I didn't know the first thing about an office. I knew a little about trucks. At least I could answer the phone. The office was right next to the depot, and the dispatcher sat in a booth where he had windows facing both ways, out into the garage and in toward us in the office. I was filing and halfway typing. And there weren't any problems about me being colored. One of the drivers was an old black man named Jake. He repaired trucks there for a lot of years, and finally they let him start driving some of the shorter runs. Taking it easy, truthful, 'cause he was getting close to retirement age, and driving was easier than working with a lot of tools doing repairs.

There were a lot of colored in Eli even then. What we called a lot. What did we know? Now there's hardly anybody else here, and that's a change I've seen with my own eyes.

It was a nice little job with that trucking company. Me and the two white women in the office got along. We liked not giving in to a lot of rough-talking men and dirt and noise while trucks came and went all day long.

But I lost the job. The way it happened just wasn't like me. But this was when I started not being sure exactly what I was like. I started changing 'til I hardly knew myself. I didn't know I was changing, or what I was changing into.

When I first came here, I was just glad to get away from Crawley. I didn't want to talk to anybody there, not even Roy. We buried Esther and Gregory and I just left on outta there. I had a little money saved up from my job at the garage. I didn't know what I was gonna do, but I told Mama I had to go. I didn't say anything to Jim. I couldn't look at him.

They sent Beetsy down to Gregory's (even if he was gone, we still called it his house) to stay with Aunt Fanny and Lyelle and Son-Son. Lyelle almost went crazy when they came and got her and told her Gregory got shot down at Ma Rhetta's. When she came down there and went up the stairs and saw the police measuring Gregory's body getting ready to take it away, she had a fit right there. She wasn't gon' let 'em take him. She didn't believe he was gone. It didn't get over to her that Esther was gone, too. Not right then. They were both full of bullets and blood—Sting Ray emptied a revolver in Esther and Gregory—but Lyelle just wasn't gon' let 'em take Gregory to the county morgue. They pulled her off him, but it was a real struggle. Aunt Fanny told me all of this later. That rascal Sting Ray got away for a little bit. But later that night the Highway Patrol picked him up about 80 miles downstate.

Mama said she blamed Jim for the shooting. But she wouldn't put him out. Everybody in Crawley, once they got to talking about it, blamed Jim. And everybody said Mama should put him out. But she wasn't about to do that. I wanted no parts of any of 'em.

So, I came here not knowing what I was doing. And come nightfall I would get lonesome and act crazy. There were some colored juke houses not far from where I lived. The colored were mostly in this one section of Eli then. Not like we live now, all over the place. But not everybody knew everybody, like in Crawley. Eli was the same distance from Chicago, but it's a truck town and it's near a steel town and a coal town, so there were a lot of single men, white and, more and more as the years went by, black. And when they'd get off of work these men would go out and drink and gamble and do all o' what men do. Cut and fight and shoot, too. Chase women, all o' that.

Well, me, a tall country girl whose hair wouldn't grow, I just had to put on dresses and makeup like everybody else. I looked ridiculous, but I didn't have anybody to compare myself with except Mama and Esther, and they never cared too much about any of that except on Sunday. So, I had a lot of catching up to do when it came to dresses.

And a lot of other things. I must have been a sight with my tall, skinny self. I looked at magazines and things and tried to look like somebody's grown woman. But I wasn't ready in my mind to act like a grown woman. I was tall, so I bought shoes with little low heels. I figured that much out. But I still looked damn funny walking in the kinda shoes I wasn't used to wearing. I wore my glasses. I put hairpins in my short hair. Sometimes I would wear funny little hair ribbons. I looked real comical, I know. But I just kept walking. Ma Rhetta used to say, "If you don't want folks dwellin' on you, Hassalia, remember, you can't see the spots on a trottin' horse. Just keep walkin', daughter, keep walkin'." In my foolish way, that's what I did.

Walked myself into trouble. I don't have to tell you it was over a man. Talk about not ready. I didn't know what I didn't know.

I would call myself going out when I would go to a juke joint. I was a fast little ol' dancer when I got going, but for the longest while nobody would ask me to dance or even talk. I didn't know how young I still looked. I was a chile, and nobody was interested in jailbait. So, I would sit there and keep time to the music and move around in my seat a little bit, and call myself having a good time. And I *was* having a good time 'cause I was *staring*, like the country fool I was. I never saw that many pretty colored men in one room. And some tough talking colored women to go with 'em. The women would kinda hang on the men, but they didn't take a lot of stuff from 'em. Get some of those gals drunk enough or mad enough and they'd pull a razor out of their purse like *that*.

I used to notice this man, nowhere near as tall as me, with slick hair, in tight, shiny suits, sporting jet black pointed-toed shoes. Had a boisterous mouth. Wore glasses. Name of Joe Boy. That's what everybody called him. I wondered how the "Boy" got on there. I heard the bartender call him a smooth-talking gambler. He never had a woman with him.

One night after he got up from playing cards he sat down at my table and said to my face, "I don't wanna take your money, and that's all I would do if we played cards. Why don't you dance with me, gal, and at least look like you're having a good time?"

I said, "Do I look to you like I'm not having a good time?"

"You could be having a better one," he said.

"I could? How?"

"First off, you could dance with me. Then you could let me take you for a little ride in my car. Maybe you saw that shiny green Mercury out front, with the tan leather interior and the whitewalls and the silver hubcaps. And then you could show me where you live so I could come around sometime and take you to dreamland."

"Dreamland? Where's that?"

He smiled and pointed to his heart.

"You're moving real fast for somebody who hasn't mentioned their name or nothing."

"You don't need to know my name, baby, to love me. Joe. Everybody calls me Joe Boy. I'm their boy, they'll all tell you, 'cause they know I'm always ready for a tight game of cards. I don't cheat anybody anywhere any time. Losers'll tell you I'm slick, but good is what I am. What's your name?"

"Hassalia."

"Hassalia." He stretched it out, like he was thinking me over. Then he said, "You're not from around here."

"No, I'm here lately."

"Where your people?"

"Over in Illinois."

"Chi?"

"No. 'Way from there."

"Where?"

"Never mind. I don't want 'em knowing I'm here."

"What, you hiding?"

"I got nothing to hide."

"You pregnant?"

"You got some nerve, Joe...Basketball Head." All of a sudden it came to me he looked like a basketball with glasses, his head was so round and brown and smooth on top of his little body.

He laughed. "Uh oh. Now I got you mad," he said. He waited a minute. "Well, are you?"

"No. If it was any business of yours."

"How long you been wearing glasses?"

"From when I was little."

"Me, too. Saved up for 'em myself. Everybody says I must be smart. You?"

"Yeah."

We just listened to Sam Cooke on the jukebox. It was "You Send Me".

"Your people gonna be coming looking for you?"

"They don't know where to look."

At first I thought it was infatuation

"I know a place you can stay if you wanna."

"I got a place to stay."

"But you're not supposed to be living in some rooming house... all alone."

"You're not the boss of me, Mister."

Honest you do, honest you do, oh oooh oooh oooh oooh oh oh oh

"Some of these gangsters around here'll do you wrong if you're not careful."

"Some of these other folks, you mean, not you?"

Whenever I'm with you

He said, "I'm not gon' do anything to mess with my game in these places. And doing women wrong will mess with my game."

"Talking about what I'm not s'posed to be doing, are you s'posed to be earning your living with a deck of cards? What does your Mama say about that?"

Mmm-huh, mmm-huh, honest you do

"Girl, I don't ask my Mama what I'm s'posed to be doing, and she doesn't ask me. If I waited on that woman, I'd still be waiting."

"What do you wanna do after you get as slick with cards

as you can get?"

"I'm nowhere near as slick as I can get. I said I was good, girl. I didn't say I was a fool. Nobody who knows about cards thinks he's that slick."

He had a big mouth, but he didn't seem like a liar or a clown, either. I said, "I bet I look to you like a country girl who wouldn't know what to say to a card dealing man. Well, you're right. I don't know what to say to you."

He laughed. "You already said it, baby. You already said it."

Little Richard came on the jukebox.

Good golly, Miss Molly. She sure likes to ball

To this day I can't tell you why I got involved with Joe Boy. He was the one who taught me the first little bit I found out about sex. He was a rough little rascal with his short self. He wasn't cruel, but he knew how to lay into a woman and wear her resistance down 'til she would do like he wanted. He showed me how I would give in to a man when I called myself not wanting to, if the man kept at me. We would meet at the juke joints and go back to his rooming house or mine. The landlady in both places didn't care one little bit. And I thought I was turning into a woman with this slick little man teaching me what I was s'posed to know. I found out a little bit about his family, how they were still in Georgia. But I never did see what was inside that man until it was too late. Joe Boy was a good gambler and real careful with his cards. He wasn't as careful with his women. What did I know? I was just one country girl. Somebody woulda told me pretty soon I wasn't the only woman he was riding around with in his green Mercury. I didn't ask anybody. I didn't wanna think about it. I would see him Saturday nights. That was all I knew to ask for. For a colored man Saturday night was a lot. And a whole lotta Saturday nights Joe Boy was with me. Nothing like that ever happened to me before.

He came by my job one day. I knew something was wrong. He never did that before. He was wearing one of his shiny suits, but it was cut up and dirty, and he was bleeding in his face. He told me he had to get outta town. Somebody was after him. I said, "But you don't cheat anybody. Who you running from?"

He said, "No, baby, I don't cheat. But not everybody believes me like you do. You got any money?" I didn't have any, and I told him.

Quicker than you could say Jack Robinson he pulled out a gun right there in the office and told Janice, one of the white women, to open the safe and give him what was in it. I begged him not to do what he was doing. But he wasn't listening to me any more. Janice opened the safe and gave him the money. And Hazel, the other white woman, just stood there with her eyes bugged out wide, scared.

Joe Boy didn't say anything to me on his way out the door. He didn't even look back.

It was months before I got the whole story about what happened to Joe Boy that day. Turned out he was keeping comp'ny with somebody else's woman. Her man had been spyin' on the two of 'em, and one day he pulled a switchblade on her—just before Joe Boy walked in. When Joe Boy tried to take the blame on himself, the man was bent and bound to cut *him*. He nicked him, but Joe Boy got away. Somebody called the police, and by the time they got there, this was the woman's story: she was home alone when *Joe Boy* came in and threatened her with a switchblade, tellin' her if she didn't leave town with him he'd scar her face—until her brave Papa came home just in time and ran bad ol' Joe Boy off. The police said they'd look for him, like they always say, and left. The man put the word on the street he was gonna fix Joe Boy for sure. So now him *and* the police were lookin' for Joe Boy.

But none of this made sense to me. I *never* saw Joe Boy

with no knife. He was a desperator from the day I met him, but he wasn't like that, I'll swear 'til today. And near as I could figure, Joe Boy thought twice about pullin' his gun to defend *this* woman, so he ran—like "a chicken tryin' not to be supper," was the way the man bragged on himself later. Joe Boy mighta been *scared*, but I don't believe he was a coward.

But I never really knew for sure. He got outta town and stayed out.

So, here were two black men, Sting Ray and Joe Boy, using guns to get what they wanted. Up 'til then I didn't even know any men with guns.

Of course I lost my job. Joe Boy stole a little over $4,000 from the trucking company, and that was enough for the folks to accuse me of being his partner. The police carried me down to the station, but after a couple of hours they could see that small town me wasn't near 'bout fast enough comp'ny for Joe Boy, and they let me go. Truthfully, they just sounded glad Joe Boy was gone, like they were pretty sure he wouldn't be showing himself back in Eli any time soon, and that was good enough for them. Black man gone.

It was a long while before I knew what to think. Joe Boy brought out the woman in me. But was he really a man, or still just a fast-talking boy? Was it man or boy who took up with a know-nothing country girl like me? Man or boy who stood up for that woman, man or boy who, a split second later, figured out she wasn't worth it—and ran for his life?

One night in my room after we made love I told him how sometimes I wanted to go home but I was scared my people would say to me, If you so grown, Hassalia, you can just *stay* gone. I told him I wasn't sure yet whether I'd left home for good or not.

He listened. Then he said, "I watched my daddy die slow, behind a mule and a plow, year by year. He died young, bent, broke, wore down, old before his time. My daddy fell to the ground one day in the hot sun. We cooled his brow and carried him in the house, but in fifteen minutes he was gone. My Mama's whole body shook. I can still hear her cryin' out, 'Weary's got a home now, Lord, just moved right on in.' She moaned all night. I'm not gonna die like that. I'm gonna die *fast*. And I'm gonna *live* fast right up to it." He turned to me. "Go home or stay here, you're not a chile any more, Hassalia." Then he kissed my forehead, rolled over and went to sleep.

I had to find something else to do. I ended up being a maid. Doing my Mama's work. Doing what her and Esther did—day work—all the time I was at home. You get tired of other people's dirt. But there's only one thing to do with it: clean it up. So, you know what to do the minute you walk into a place.

And, too, being a maid, cleaning woman, whatever you wanna call me, you get to see white folks up close when they don't know you're looking. People look right through a maid after a while. Like you're not there. Their children come and talk to you, for a little while, 'cause you listen. But you know you can't raise these children all over again. And they don't know how to tell their folks they're not happy, which some of these white children truthfully are not. I understand that. A chile in pain is a chile in pain. I've learned that over the years. I don't fault the young, white or black. They're children. They're looking to us older folks to show them how to do. We can't tell 'em how scared we are, too, just like they are. We don't want 'em to get so scared they can't move. But how do you tell a chile to be brave when you know there's a whole lot out there for him to be scared of? Well, the chile don't wanna hear that anyway, even if you could find a way to tell 'em.

I didn't know anything about this right then, you understand. I had to learn it. I had to work as a maid and take myself back to Crawley time by time to see Mama and Aunt

Fanny and the rest of 'em—even Jim, with his slow eyes looking cautious as a cat all of his days. I had to figure out why I wouldn't stay there. I wouldn't. After I'd go see the folks, I'd come right back to dirty, noisy Eli. There were colored aplenty. And the church. Which I came to, finally. For comfort, shelter from the storm. Folks who are sure about how they stand with God are a lot surer than me. I do a lot of listening in church. And just enough praying when I get home to make me feel like I'm ready for the Lord when He wants to talk to me. But I'll never tell you I'm a holy woman. Or a good Christian.

Not too long after Joe Boy left outta here, I met Rev. And I'm with him still. For now. Been a lot of years between us. And we've got Johnnie, our son.

The way that all came about was like this. After what happened with Joe Boy, I was some kinda famous around there. I don't think folks thought I was for real "dangerous". But Joe Boy wasn't there any more, and I was. And they saw how him and me were running around together. And they were asking themselves how this skinny gal got hold to this dangerous little man and kept him for a while.

When he came on my job robbing and carrying on, some folks thought I musta been in on the thing with him. I tried to tell people he wasn't thinking about taking me with him. He was a desperator all the time he knew me. He covered it up so I wouldn't see it. Then when it came time to move fast, when he was in trouble for sure, he cut me loose. And all the time he was with me he was with somebody else's woman. I don't know how I didn't look like a fool to everybody. I felt like one.

So, one evening there I was, sitting back in one of those clubs, feeling like a fool but looking like something else to folks. This tall, nice-looking man came up and talked to me. That was Rev. He wasn't the kinda man who went to that kinda place regular. He was there with some gentlemen

friends of his. He felt real uncomfortable. We started talking and next thing I knew he was seeing me home. He left me real nice at the door and didn't do anything out of the way. He didn't even say anything about calling again. "Good night, ma'm." Real gentle.

That was Rev, right from the get. A real gentle man. Just what I needed. There was a whole lot of devilment in me I didn't know about. I didn't see it for devilment right then, but that's what it was. I stayed mad at a whole lot of folks for a long time.

I was mad at Mama for what she did with Jim. For not putting him out after her brother and her daughter died 'cause of him. I was mad at Sting Ray, Lord knows, but at least he went to jail. I was mad at Jim for bringing all of this mess down on everybody just 'cause his manhood told him he could. It took me a while to see I was mad at Daddy, too, 'cause he was the one who left me there with all of these confused folks.

Then I met Rev. Sweet man. Kind man. And he told me we were gonna get married. He was tall like me, thin like me. Lonesome like me. His people were all gone, though. His Mama and Daddy and a bunch of 'em died off in a bad fever—just cut through 'em all like a sickle. Rev was the only one left. He started roaming the roads. He wasn't but eleven. Eating what he could find or beg. Bummed 'til he was almost a man. Then he got taken to by some railroad folks who showed him how to work in the yard. Hauling, loading and unloading. Hard work. But it kept him strong, him with his long, tall back. I looked on that back and the muscles in it many a time and said, "Lord, now that's what a strong man looks like, anybody wanna know."

He was called "Rev" from when he was a chile, 'cause he was always the quiet, serious one, the Reverend. His Mama and then his Daddy and then the rest of 'em all took to calling him Rev. His name is Chester. But everybody calls

him Rev. And when he said he wanted to marry me, I didn't know what to think. I was still nothing but a gal. I had filled out a little bit and thought I had some stuff to show. And maybe I did, a little bit. I was foolish, but I was brave, too. Sometimes there's not a whole lot of difference. For me it was brave to put on a dress and keep it on and try to act like a grown woman. Rev made me wanna keep doing that. After Daddy and Jim and Sting Ray I wasn't sure what a grown man was, or what a grown woman was s'posed to be like. That's what I'm still learning. Now. When there isn't much time left to do much learning.

So, me and Rev had Johnnie. I named him that. Rev said he didn't mind. If that's what I wanted to call the boy, it was fine with him. And Johnnie's been what's kept us going. Rev's slowed down. The railroad was good to him; they lightened up his work load. And they cut him back to three days a week. That's about as much as he can do now. I've been working steady all of these years, so we've got a little put by. I know it's not enough for him and Johnnie both. He's gon' need the boy's help. And I know Johnnie's gon' do right by him. There just isn't any other way.

It seems like we were just getting started. And then I started to feeling real weak all of a sudden. I know I've been working too hard some of these years when we were first buying this little house. I wanted to do so much. Fix it up nice, you know. Which we did. But I just wouldn't stop working. And when I first started feeling poorly, real weak, I thought I just needed to slow down. I'm a young woman, I said to myself, I've got a long way to go. Johnnie's got to go to college. And on and on like that. I was just thinking and planning. Nobody was gon' stop *me*.

Then the doctor told me what it is. Leukemia. My blood won't act right. There's nothing they can do. My time's come. I've got to let Rev and Johnnie go. Say goodbye. Die. When I'm not ready to go. But here it is. My time. And I've

got to do what Ma Rhetta said she couldn't, put away the cares of the day.

It's hard, let me tell you. Johnnie's sixteen now. He's just starting to grow into himself. He's a fine-looking boy. Loves basketball. He's got hair all over his head like the children do these times, calling it a natural or an Afro. It looks to me like he needs a haircut, but I'm long past fighting with the boy over that. These young folks today are carrying on, talking black and proud like they do. I don't know where it all came from, but I know it had to come.

That fall I left outta Crawley and came here to Eli, I would see on the news on the TV the young folks at Central High School in Little Rock. I saw those nice, well-dressed young folks trying to go to school. National Guard and everybody else trying to get 'em in. Because they were colored the white folks didn't want 'em. It scared me, don't ask me to lie. It took the National Guard when some of us wanted to put something in our heads.

It's a long time from those young folks—I wasn't much older than they were—to Johnnie. But that's where we are today. I don't know where we're gon' be tomorrow. I won't be there to see it. Johnnie will. And Rev. Not me. But I feel good about the time now. Good about what's happening. Two books I keep by my bed these times. Lay 'em down to talk to Rev or Johnnie, and to one or two of my church folks come by to see me regular. And the minister, Reverend Cobb.

But the rest of the time I stay in my Bible and I read my *Roots*. That Alex Haley, he did something when he wrote that one, yessir. He wrote that *Autobiography of Malcolm X*, too, and that was another good one. That Malcolm was a pistol, a man of the folks all the time, even when he didn't know it. But Detroit Red was the same man who ended up going to Mecca. The same man. Folks don't wanna see it. But the one man was inside the other one. Like Paul on the

road to Damascus. He got struck with what he had to do, and nobody could stop him. 'Til they killed him. Him and Dr. King. Malcolm wasn't gon' let go. Him nor Dr. King. Not until they got to the holy places. The path isn't the one we choose. It's the one we follow. That's what I'm doing. Looking for the holy place. I believe it's right here around me. All I've got to do is find it. Alex Haley did it up mighty proud when he wrote this *Roots*. He got the story of all of us into that one. And when they put it on TV, I'm telling you, you couldn't get the three of us away from that set. All week long. And everywhere you went through the day folks white and black weren't talking about anything else. "She said... and then he said...and then *I* said..." Lord, that's all folks talked about. We had a little bit of this nation's attention that week. I was so glad to live to see that. It was only a week, I know. But there was no way anybody could turn it off. Folks who were watching it couldn't help themselves. White folks especially. They wanted to know the story. And here they are, all mixed up in the story, and acting like it's ours. Like they didn't have but a little bit to do with it. Talking about, "No, not me, not my folks, not my people, we didn't treat you black folks like that." They already forgot about 1957, and Central High School.

That's what I keep thinking Johnnie and his friends are gon' find out. Just how it's been for all o' us, and what we gon' do to turn this thing around and make it better for colored folks. What I don't know how to tell Johnnie is how to understand what happened to me and my folks. He's been with me back to Crawley. Mama spoils him real good when he's there. She can get real silly about Johnnie. He doesn't really look like his Uncle Johnnie who he's never met. So, he doesn't carry Mama back like that. She just likes him 'cause he's mine and she didn't believe I'd ever have a big ol' boy of my own when I didn't know how to act like any kinda girl when I left her and her house. I had a lot of learning to do away from Crawley, but I can't say I got too far.

The three of us went South and saw some of Rev's raising places. Came a time there 'mongst the trees, it was so beautiful dark and green, we were riding along in the car and I was just lost in how pretty and green and dark it was down South. I didn't see what was happening. Johnnie either. He was in the back seat staring out the window and I was in the front seat doing the same thing. Both of us from up north didn't know about heat just like this and green just like this and hills and twists and turns in the road, and big rivers and little cricks to cross over. How lost somebody could get in all o' that if they wanted to. How would they ever get found, was what I was thinking.

And, sudden like, Rev just pulled the car off the road and put his head down in his hands and started crying like a baby. He couldn't stop. He had to get out and walk by himself. I stayed in the car with Johnnie. "Is Daddy all right? What's wrong with Daddy?" he kept asking me. I said, "Yes, honey, Daddy's all right. Daddy's just a little sad now. He's thinking about his folks he left down here when he was little. They're not here now, like me and Daddy are with you. He misses 'em, is all."

That's what I was telling the boy—he was eight at the time—but I was trying to tell myself, too, what was happening to my husband. What all happened just for him to get to Eli a grown man. And marry me. And for us to have Johnnie. What was hurting him was, he didn't have his folks to show none of it to.

He got back in the car and said to me, "Please, can we go back home now?" I said, "Sure, baby, I'm ready to go when you are. Aren't you ready to go back home, darling?" I was talking to Johnnie. He said all he wanted was to get back home to his bicycle. So we turned the car around right there and drove without stopping right back here to Eli.

We went out to California once, to take Johnnie to Disneyland. He loved that. But California wasn't any place we wanted to stay. We came back here to Eli after that, too.

Eli isn't pretty. But it's where me and Rev stood still together for a time. It's where I found out what it is to love a man—Rev. And where he found out what loving a woman could bring to him—me and Johnnie. When he didn't think he'd ever have any folks ever again, he got us. And now him and Johnnie are going on.

And they got people beyond me—my folks in Crawley—I keep telling him. He doesn't wanna see it like that. He wants me to know he doesn't want me to go. I understand that. I appreciate what the man's saying. I love him 'cause he says it. But Johnnie's got people and I don't want 'em forgotten.

Mama's still in Crawley. And Jim. Still in that house. To tell you the honest to God truth, I don't know if they ever did what I saw 'em doing again. Maybe they did. Lord knows folks talk like they did. But that doesn't mean it's true. It may a just been Ma Rhetta dying that pushed Mama and Jim at each other. Maybe not. Maybe they were doing that time by time for a lot of years, and kept it up. Mama said they didn't, but what if she was lying to me?

I do know a couple a years after I left Crawley Jim got a regular girlfriend who used to come out to Crawley and see him. She'd stay there at the house. Name of Carmilla. Carmilla was a dresser, let me tell you, a real sport. Played the horses and all. Fast living, good-looking woman. She was particular about Jim, but Jim, or anybody with good sense, didn't think he was the only man she had.

For one thing, the first time she came to Crawley she brought one with her. He was funny, I'll give you that. A big fat ol' sissy who went by the name of Dumpling. Her particular friend, and nobody better say anything about it. Real dapper he was, too. Rings on his fingers. Fine shoes.

187

Carried a walking stick and gloves. A colored gentleman you mighta called him, if he wasn't funny acting. Like he favored the company of men. What were him and Carmilla doing together was what everybody wanted to know. They were real tight. She didn't hardly travel anywhere without him. Folks finally got to saying he was pimping for her. But then Jim wouldna stood for that but so long, and him and Carmilla were friendly for six, seven years.

There came a time when Jim and Carmilla started talking about getting married. Course nobody knew how serious Carmilla coulda been. She loved a good time too much, seemed like, to ever think about marrying anybody. Turned out Carmilla wasn't thinking about marrying Jim or anybody else. But he was acting like he wanted to marry her. Was he saying that just to upset Mama's world?

Well, he sure did. Mama had a fit. Carried on. Fell out. I saw her during some of it, when Jim was back and forth talking like he was gon' marry Carmilla and then like he wasn't and then back like he was. Mama was half crazy. She would talk about everything else: the church folks, her stories on the TV, whatever white folks she was working for right then. But she wasn't thinking about anything but whether Jim was gon' marry Carmilla and leave her there in that house with nothing but Ma Rhetta to think about and how Esther and Gregory died there. And me and Johnnie gone for sure. And Daddy Izell never coming back.

But I don't think Jim was being as evil as folks said. I think he was just looking out for Jim, looking to see what he could make for himself before he got too old. Just Jim, wanting to do it all, or thinking he could do it all, with any woman he wanted, any time he wanted. And nail down a fine-looking woman like Carmilla. Jim was chuckling, that was for sure.

But, it turned our Carmilla wasn't about to get married. She didn't wanna give up the high life and stay with one man. Jim pleasured her. But so did a lot of men. Living good was what Carmilla liked. Not living good with Jim. And Jim musta found that out. I wonder how he took it. It turned out he stayed right there in Crawley, in that house, with Mama. They're there still. The two of 'em. Used to being talked about. Used to each other. I go there and I come back. I can't stay. I don't understand either one of 'em.

Aunt Fanny stayed on there with Lyelle. They're still there. Son-Son is grown and in school getting ready to make himself a lawyer. Big, smart, fine man, crazy about his Mama. He stays close. And he kept her all these years from being too mad at Jim for bringing it all down, causing Gregory to get shot like that.

Beetsy stayed there with 'em 'til she got married. She moved to New York, her and her husband. They've got three children. Beetsy will come to Crawley but hate every minute of it. She brings the children for Mama to see. She just doesn't talk about Esther and Sting Ray. I know she's been to see him in prison. I don't know what she said to him.

M'Lady got taken for what folks believed she was, but we didn't wanna hear: a white woman who wasn't right in her mind. The asylum folks finally came and got her from out of Mama's house. The folks that left her were old themselves. Her sister and brother. Both of them weren't long for this world when Ma Rhetta and Mama heard tell of her and took her in. Got so nobody asked Mama about it, not the county or anybody, 'cause they didn't know what to do with her either. Her brother and sister had already died one right behind the other. So, she didn't have anybody. Ma Rhetta and Mama just took her in, feeling sorry for her. I can tell you truthful, I never heard Mama complain about M'Lady being there. Not once. What was there to complain about? She didn't say anything 'til after Ma Rhetta died. And then I heard her talk. But I couldn't really make sense of it right then. I've been listening hard to her words ever since that

189

time. Listening to 'em still. M'Lady was a good soul. She was trapped, being old and not having anybody, to where it looked like she was crazy. To me, it looks like that's when she *went* crazy. But I don't believe that old woman was crazy. She made sense to me. Nobody wanted her. That didn't mean she was crazy. She went crazy to get outta being somebody nobody wanted.

Aunt Fanny never did go anything like crazy again. She had enough of those asylum places. She'd stay six months, come out, go back six months more, come back out. It went like that for years. After Esther and Gregory died, she musta known Lyelle and Son-Son needed her. She got right and stayed right. Is to this day. She's my sweet ol' sister now, my Aunt Fanny. Couldna made it through the storm without her. She was light when there was nothing but darkness closing around me at Mama's house. Or was it—is it—Ma Rhetta's house? I still can't make up my mind.

It turned out Johnnie—my brother Johnnie—got to New York. I found out from some piano player passing through one of those little dives here in Eli. He knew Johnnie. I asked him to tell me the truth. And I believed him. He said Johnnie came to New York and wanted to sing and play piano.

But he couldn't play good enough to get work doing that. There were a lot of good players around. And sing? He said, truth to tell, Johnnie wasn't that much. He would get up and sing one song and it would be all right. But then he'd go on to the next one and he couldn't keep going, couldn't keep believing what he was singing. And nobody else could, either. Said Johnnie was pretty—I knew that—and that's what got him into trouble. He took up with women who wanted him just 'cause he was pretty. They started using him just to show him off to other women. When they got tired of him they dumped him fast. He wore out. The man said there was talk Johnnie was so pretty he got to be a punk for some man. But the man said he didn't believe it and I told him I didn't either. If he did, that wasn't Johnnie. He said Johnnie got mixed up with some folks using heroin, and Johnnie got on it, too. Got into it bad, fell in with folks who weren't doing anything but that. And then the man lost track of him. Didn't hear tell of him any more. He said, "I'm sorry to be the one to tell you all of this about your brother. He wasn't a bad kid. But there were a lot of fine looking young colored men in New York trying to make it. Music. Sex. Heroin. It all got to be too much for a lot of 'em. They forgot why they came. And they got outta touch with their families. That's what happened to Johnnie. He was a nice looking kid. But what did he want there? To sing or to be pretty and have a good time with a fine woman on his arm everywhere he went? Did he know, do you think?" I told him yes, hell, yes, Johnnie knew what he wanted. He wanted to sing like Nat King Cole and Sam Cooke. The man said to me, "Yeah, him and 40, 50 other colored kids getting off the bus every week. You ask Nat King Cole and Sam Cooke how they sing like they do, and they couldn't tell you. They just take care of it, is all. Johnnie didn't take care of what little bit he had."

I couldn't argue with the man. I wasn't there. Johnnie couldn't stay in Crawley, but he couldn't make it away from there, either. The world was bigger and badder than he knew. It swallowed him up, damn it. Wish I'da known. Maybe I could have helped him to be all right, even if he couldn't sing like Nat King Cole. Be Johnnie.

But I couldn't. So, I got this Johnnie. And Rev. And my *Roots*. And my Bible.

And I gotta die.

I think about Ma Rhetta most of all now. She was a hard ol' girl, but she's tender to me. She looked after us the best she knew how. She hurt Mama and Jim and Aunt Fanny and Gregory a lot, 'cause she didn't know how to hold 'em close. I don't think she thought she could, counta they came from daddies who didn't wanna stay with her. The daddies were the ones who did the missing out. But try to teach a man that.

I feel like I'm going to join Ma Rhetta now. I'm stepping into the stream, like M'Lady said, of those who are remembered. And just like we found out from the asylum folks M'Lady's real name was Melody, the stream doesn't tell anybody how deep it is, or how cold. You gotta get in it.